FOR CLAUDIA

Also available from Road Junky Guides

The Road Junky Travel Handbook

Does your guide tell you how to travel the world with no money, fool immigration officials or bluff your way through teaching an English class with no qualifications?

Or will your guidebook let you know the craziest places in the world to travel, how to make a living on the road and the best places to get stoned once you've saved up enough?

In an age of consumer travel where people think experience is something they can buy, Road Junky shows you how to get on the road and stay there. With travel tips, insights and info from decades of hard traveling, the Road Junky Handbook is uncensored, irreverent and edgier than any other guide out there.

We reveal:

- how to hitchhike anywhere
- 101 ideas to work around the world
- the best parties to be found on the planet
- how to avoid the world's most clever travel scams
- Enough guides, stories and tips to make you quit your day job and get on the road for as long as you can handle it.

Coming Soon from Road Junky

Eating Air in India
by Robin Brown

The most authentic book on India you'll ever read, Written by a man with decades of experience of traveling around the subcontinent, hanging out with holy men, dodging police and bandits and getting to know the secret India that never makes it into print.

Traveling variously barefoot and by motorbike, Eating Air in India is at once a travel classic and an accomplished anthropological work.

Now Available from Road Junky

Hand to Mouth to India
by Tom Thumb

Tom was 20 years old, broke and wanted to go to India. So he packed up his clarinet, toothbrush and sleeping bag and hitch-hiked there with no money at all.

Braving hunger, deserts, amoebas and rape attempts by frustrated truck drivers, Tom followed in the footsteps of the original hippies and arrived in Goa with less than a dollar to his name.

"I bet this guy never worked a day in his life." Howard Marks

JAMES

by Thomas Thirkell

PUBLISHED BY ROADJUNKY

Published by Road Junky Guides

www.roadjunky.com
Editor@roadjunky.com

ISBN 0-9795984-1-9

IN THE MIDDLE OF LIFE
I ENTERED A DARK WOOD

"nel mezzo del cammin di nostra vita,
mi ritrovai per una selva oscura"
—Dante

with some people there is too much past

CHAPTER ONE: JAMES 4:05AM LONDON: THE 16TH OF JUNE

It's like she was always there.

Pacing up and down the floorboards of my attic room.

Outside the comfortable lights of west London warm the darkness, reassuring me after the primeval morass of my waking dreams, that they are not real, concrete, and can easily be dispersed. I stare down at the empty street below, so busy in the day, its evenly spaced lamp-posts, well laid paving – and through the open window I hear the soft hum of electronics and a gentle breeze rustling up the hill.

Suddenly I feel good to be alive, thankful for this too too solid flesh – I stretch, shivering slightly, pull on a jumper and walk to the fridge and open it – its light gently illuminates the kitchen so I leave it open.

I go back to the polished wood floor of the front room, sit in a cold armchair; the fridge starts up its hum; I watch the trickle of its light casting itself tentatively across the furniture, wall and floor nearest to the kitchen door, and happy in that moment of stasis let time flow as one long moment, my mind resting on the still, revealed night world around me. The cat walks in and brushes her tail against me, I reach down a hand and feel her flowing form escape me – it is time to go back to bed until morning, I guess.

◆ ◆ ◆ ◆ ◆ ◆

The refrigerator is still humming, still the loudest noise amongst the small background sounds of night, but muffled by its travel down the corridor from the kitchen and through my ajar bedroom door. The dim light in the bedroom is dappled from the leaves on the tree between the houses at the back, backlit only by the diffuse glow of the London sky, a softer light than that at the front of the house.

I stir in my bed. The clock reads 4:27, somehow a comforting time, well before the first morning delivery van, rushing alone across Campden Hill, and well after the last party revelers (falling down it).

But somehow I can't get to sleep, not that I am disenjoying just lying there, in tranquility, my thoughts moving swiftly with the leaves of the tree playing their shadow dance dream across the white walls of my bedroom.

Slowly thoughts turn, and I think on Madeleine, her solitary figure walking proudly but blindly up the High Street, her nose tipped up so slightly, her lips ready to utter a friendly greeting should she chance upon an acquaintance, or even ready to smile at a passer-by. I find it pleasant to rest my thought on my friend, Madeleine, and follow her in my imagination into a shop, where she may purchase, what? some ribbon for her new chiffon cover for her… I let her wander around the store – whom shall she encounter, which friend or acquaintance? or shall I let her walk home, a freshly purchased novel under her arm, to her pretty flat in Chelsea, where she can make tea and complain gently about her love life, and the deficiencies of so and so, and how worried she is by it all, so after all it is time for a glass of wine, is it not?

Then my mind shifts scene, and I am sitting at the small checkered table clothed table of a café in France or Spain. Nowhere really. And in walks Justine, all sex and curves, her dark hair dashing out from her headscarf, her rouged lips glistening into a smile; and she sits down and crosses her legs athletically, snaps out a cigarette, lights it and inhales.

"So what is the matter?" I ask her; her smile broadens but she doesn't answer, and I am floating, floating up, floating above fields and trees and houses, and in the distance is the sea-shore, and on it the cafés and palm trees, and I am diving towards nirvana and splash…

The phone wakes me.

Rapidly, before answering, I take in that it is daytime, part sunny, part cloudy, cool, probably about nine from the sound of the traffic and the slant of the insipid sunlight; ring; hadn't meant to sleep so late; ring; perhaps it was the middle night sojourn that had tired me…

On the third ring I picked up, cut the impinging sound, and managed a strangled hello into the receiver.

"Well Madeleine, hello!" I say in answer to the familiar voice.

"You sound surprised," she says.

I quickly try to decide whether to give her the true explanation for the sound of surprise in my voice, which was inadvertent, coming from within the layer of dreamland I had just woken from. I give up and change the subject.

"…and how are you this morning?"

"Oh, fine," she drawls in her southern lilt, so charming when she is talking about the right things, ordinary things, nice things, reassuring things – I imagine her brushing back her hair with one hand as she says: "You want to come round for coffee?"

I ponder, more for affect than out of any indecision: for of course, I would.

Anything to fill this emptiness. Even this.

So in the relative passivity of mid-morning, in the slant of sun cutting through running cloud, the noisy passage of traffic churning past me, spoiling the air of the narrow street with their stinging fumes, under the trees, their leaves a simulacrum of the Eden we will never know, I walk over Campden Hill, across the High Street, and walk the salubrious streets of Chelsea with their solid airs and graces, to finally deposit myself at the shiny front door of the small terraced house where Madeleine will shortly be brewing coffee for me, and complaining, and making me feel at home, if only for the moment…

◆ ◆ ◆ ◆ ◆ ◆

Madeleine's drawing room peers out of the triple bay window onto a short street of similar houses opposite, mid-Victorian, old enough to have small trees sprouting from the unreachable cornices around their higher windows; enough sky is visible for the view to remain open, though the street is not too wide, and the architecture of the houses, though plain, is well proportioned enough and with sufficient detail to lend charm to the scene.

Inside, the first thing to notice is the easel casually display-ing a watercolour of another interior, painted by Madeleine, similar but strangely not the same as the one one is standing in, for there is a lot of standing in Madeleine's drawing-room as you shall see, which add a mirror depth to her carefully constructed interior.

Not that the room gives the impression of being carefully arranged; rather, it has a bohemian air, which flows easily from the easel and the oil paint tubes and brushes in a jar on the table in front of the window, to the books apparently stacked haphazard on their green, wooden shelves. But on closer inspection it may be discovered that the books have been purposely arranged in this haphazard way, some on their sides, stacked, some mixed with magazines in piles on the floor so a coffee or drinks tray may be casually placed atop. And then one discovers, if one cares for books, that the titles and editions are mostly of impeccable pedigree, though the covers may be slightly scuffed and the leaves dog-eared in places.

That early summer morning a fire was burning merrily in the grate, and Madeleine was reclined on the sofa busy on a phone conversation; she waved me to sit in a gesture that at the same time bade me feel at ease: coffee? she mouthed silently as her conversor spoke.

I retreated to the tiny kitchen with its large window that overlooked a blossoming cherry tree, and sat on the uncom-fortable garden style banquette as the coffee brewed under its hiss of gas in the espresso machine.

From the drawing room I could hear Madeleine banter in her southern drawl, then another silence as her conver-sation continued. Outside the morning was turning towards noon and the quality of light had changed, thickened, and the background roar of the city, noticeable even from this garden perch at the back of the house, was noticeably heavier, denser, even if not louder.

I fell to thinking of the novel I was writing, and how I would construct it – I had scarcely begun the latest attempt: but I imagined it could be along the lines of somebody's journey round the environs of London, a personal journey, an inner voyage delineated by outer space.

But the familiar frustration grasped me so I almost felt my face redden, my pulse quicken – I sympathized with Madeleine all of a sudden, her half finished oils, her easel unused for a year now, only a couple of sketches attempted. To create is to thrust against the leaden weight of society, its conformity, concreteness, density; and it is to deny the constant tumble of life from the now into the future – to hold the vision is all, especially for a painter, I thought to myself; though for a writer there is somehow more leeway, as though the written word is ahistorical, and the written thought may be interrupted, then continued at any time...

I let the view from the window distract me from my reverie, the hard corners of the backs of houses up the row of the side street, the stunted trees in the small, cramped back gardens, and the sky flowing anonymously above.

I poured the coffee and took it through with a second cup for Madeleine to the drawing room. She was still conversing, waving her free arm around, taking succour from the idle banter she was engaged in.

I sit in the small open side armchair with its faux Louis Sixteenth classical motif material and carved wooden arms and legs, beside the fire with its small dancing flames, though it is cold neither outside nor in the room, and sip the bitter espresso from its small delicate cup, wondering whether to bother to add more sugar or not. I cross my legs. I pick up a book and leaf through its title pages; a pleasing American edition of Ulysses. I leaf through to the beginning of part two and read its opening pages, about pussums and his (or her) bowl of milk, and the man giving it to her, Bloom, Leopold Bloom, and cooking his wife her breakfast and carrying it up to her, Molly I suppose, and it is all very immediate, graphically here and now, so much so that the grand old master makes my hair start to stand on end, so miraculous is his rendition of the scene: like those childhood memories of moments so complete that their texture and every nuance can be felt whenever recalled, though seldom rendered by art or into a sympathetic recall by any reader...

"James, how are you?" Madeleine has replaced the receiver without me noticing. I shift my gaze from my inner thought and focus on Madeleine – her form so vivid in the sudden beam of sunlight that is falling through the glass of the slightly open window.

◆ ◆ ◆ ◆ ◆ ◆

Flashing blue light of ambulance blaring past, freezing the street into an alienated blur; cars part and re-assemble in its cumbersome wake. I tuck the milk Madeleine has sent me out to buy from the corner shop deeper into my coat pocket, lest it drop out, break and spill.

Madeleine has taken to her bed, a sudden migraine having driven her from the sofa to the more secure fastness of her small bedroom with its large window. I sit down on the corner of the foot of the small four poster that fits into her room as a small box inside a slightly larger one. Up on top of the panelled, fitted, cream painted wardrobes lie hatboxes: does anyone wear hats any more, does Madeleine? James searches his mind and finds he cannot picture his dear friend in a hat except in his imagination; there she walks in the sunlight, flouncing, a younger Madeleine, all ribbons and gaiety, trees in blossom, and a large hat sat jauntily above her dark curling locks, on her pale, freckled face a laughing smile.

The image fades and James is sitting on the foot of her bed again; outside the sun must have gone behind a cloud again, for the back gardens seen through the large window darken, their colours fleeing as fast as the image that had been so clear in his mind just a moment before.

His thought was broken by the ring of the doorbell.

"Go and answer it for me, hon."

He did, rising from Madeleine's bed, opening the door a crack as he retreated back to his position on the bed so the unexpected visitor could be received in situ, the tableau undisturbed, entering it as it were as the eye enters a picture.

"Hello," boomed a voice.

Before the bulk of the body to which it belonged could enter the bedroom, James knew to whom it belonged: the tall, rotund figure of Montagu Withnail Smith loomed before his inner eye.

"In here," Madeleine called.

The front door was slammed to, the bedroom door opened wider and a large head peered in from its top, a waistcoated stomach protruded past its middle, and at the foot of the door a pair of smartly booted feet.

"Good morning to you, both," intoned the great Montagu, and entered the rest of his bulk into the room. Squeezing between the bed and the TV at its foot, he passed round to the window side of the bedroom.

"Sit down, sit down," said Madeleine, patting the covers near her left hand; to which injunction Montagu merely nodded his assent, for he had been about to anyway, and as he lowered his ample posterior onto the ancient springs beneath it, the whole apparatus: springs, covers, posts – sagged precariously and emitted loud, complaining squeaking rasps as though near to death.

"Now where is Ruben?"

"That smelly dog," Montagu pressed his lips, looking disdainful, but his coal black eyes were laughing.

"Ruben! Ruben!" called Madeleine, and the little smelly dog she loved came trotting in, blinking from another nap he had been taking in an undisturbed part of the flat, jumped up on the bed and curling up immediately closed his eyes to resume his slumber.

"Now my morning is complete!" beamed Madeleine.

Montagu Withnail Smith: what could I not say about him – that he was large, larger than life; that he had a deep melodious voice that issued forth from his small round mouth framed by red full lips like a rosebud's as though by a miracle – or a mistake: for one expected so sweet a mouth set in its long pale face broken by an aquiline nose, the black curls falling foppishly but not too rakishly over an intelligent forehead – one might have expected the voice of a robin, a chirping, the kind of voice that accompanies a rubbing together of the hands, apologetic, even wheedling. But no rubbing of the hands in supplication of his audience apart from sometimes in jest, from Montagu Withnail Smith. His arms did tend to rotate around his elbows, in small gestures, his fine hands parting the air like the wings of a bird, his long fingers adding expression and emphasis, rather than his shoulders – but this might have been due to his large size, an attempt to limit the scope of his gestures in the confined spaces of polite society, rather than any innate sense of timidity, an emotion somewhat foreign to one Monty!

"Some coffee, Monty?" drawled Madeleine. She was recumbent now, a posture of vulnerability she was want to adopt when she wished to elicit sympathy. Montagu obliged her immediately:

"Let me fetch you another pillow and get the coffee myself!" And soon he was returned, and Madeleine propped up and smiling wanly her eyes watery and mystical, and Montagu sat next to her sipping coffee, delicately for so large a man, from a small cup, replacing it carefully back on its saucer held in his other hand between each sip, and I, James, still sat where I had been when the doorbell had first rung – and an air of permanence descended on the scene, the dog curled on the flowered cover, as though we had all entered the still world of an old oil painting, or were sitting still as stone as the world spun recklessly beneath us...

◆ ◆ ◆ ◆ ◆ ◆

Such timeless moments rarely last for long (indeed, by definition they cannot, being outside time, so to speak) – the nature of the timeless is defined by its brevity – as a full stop or a point only symbolically occupies space, the timeless moment only symbolically occupies time – it does not exist in clock time, even atomic clock time – yet within such a moment rests the eternal. Paradise, or one form of it in the eternal now, is merely a succession of such moments; yet how do they succeed each other, join together, one to the next, isolated as they are in their perfections (by magic?)... yet they can, they do, in those seldom experienced but long remembered golden afternoons that occur from time to time in our long lives (too seldom, too seldom).

The sun came out from behind its cloud, the back gardens lit up in brilliant greens and Montagu sipped his last sip of coffee and replacing the cup on saucer placed the ensemble on a handy side table.

He sighed and stretching out his arms pulled back his jacket sleeves so his large, blue enameled cufflinks were exposed. He ruffled back his hair with one of his long fingered hands –

"So what are we doing today?"

The question was addressed to both myself and Madeleine, rather than himself; there was no hint in his question that the three of us might embark on some expedition that very day or that he might do something with both or either of us, though it left a delicious faint hint of his involvement in our lives: Montagu, his personality invariably flamboyant, his motivation a mystery, carried that mixture of promised excitement with the reassurance of a large intelligence, that was intoxicating to us both.

Madeleine smiled at Montagu.

" I have to visit John Sandoe's; he has a book or two in for me I ordered some time ago, I just haven't had the time or energy to go – will you come with me James?"

" Now!" I gasped, almost spluttering: my plans for the day were so barely formed I did not want to straight away commit myself: good friend that she was and seeing my plight Madeleine said:

" Well, I'm not sure I have the strength, but let's see, it is a nice day outside."

And John Sandoe's bookshop was only a few blocks walk away.

I allowed the invitation to rest the while by answering with a quiet perhaps, although I began to favour the idea, and was searching through my to do list and looking for gaps in the necessities, while Madeleine and Montagu chatted amiably about this and that.

I left my post on the bed and left them chatting and sat myself back in the chair by the fire of the front drawing-room.

There, through the distant murmur of their pleasant voices, in the vacancy of the room, I could think.

And in that room, now empty of Madeleine's form reclining on the sofa, and quiet from the incessant chatter of her voice on the telephone, only the odd car hissing past almost silently outside, the sky now a uniform blue, only the shifting flames of the fire changing their formless patterns to mark the passage of time – I allowed my mind to sink into a repose and then to wander.

When one speaks of the mind wandering one normally means its ranging over the past or forays into the future, or even over fantastical versions of both or either; but I, rather, let my imagination feel the present, let my mind follow my thoughts only as they crossed over from the past into the future, or visa versa – and again I fell into the wonderful sensation of thus inhabiting the eternal now, a timeless space between past and future, and privately I blessed Madeleine the sanctuary of her flat, where such moments could so much more easily come into existence than most other environments I frequented.

It was the odd mixture, so carefully thought out and so impossible to plan, of sociability and privacy, formality and laissez-faire that she had achieved partly through her lassitude, and partly through the generosity of her imagination.

The murmur of voices next door continues, making me feel drowsy; the fire crackles, its heat warming into a deep relaxation. Although I don't close my eyes the room disappears, becomes a virtual tableau, a still life template I can freely imprint my mind upon (with the flora and fauna of my imagination).

Images range from the purely imaginary: landscapes I have never trodden, people I have never met, expanding galaxies of solar systems multi-coloured and multi-layered – to the factually banal; I see my cat licking her paws, my front room, in shade now it is midday, the sun streaming in through the bedroom at the back. I see my mother in her red straw hat, the unlikely gardener and my wife that was, smiling up at me, also gardening, a memory garnered from a photograph I had often seen but could no longer remember – and then a moment of confusion seized me, panic almost, as though I could no longer disentangle the truth from the fiction, what had happened from what I thought had happened, what I had seen from what I visually constructed from the parts looted from the storehouse of my memory.

So shocked out of my unified reverie, the happy dream moment shattered, the room comes back into focus as a room; the titles on the book covers, the scuffed corner of the sofa, the tick of the mantelpiece clock... and back into focus came the voices of my friends: Madeleine and Montagu – his booming voice relating a yarn to do with a lady and a dog and Madeleine was laughing...

I slink off, passing through the dark corridor, clicking the door behind me with a gentle push, and I was (am?) in the street, in the sunlight and away from the thoughts I had been having in Madeleine's flat, and away from the conversation on the bed that she was having with Montagu.

The day was at its zenith, bright and shadows short; I jaunted my stride and headed for the Beach – down Redcliffe Gardens with its deadly stream of traffic heading south inexorably as a river down a canyon, its high sided period houses gloomily brooding over their heritage; turned left along west-east leading Tregunter Road, where the houses loosened up their limbs to become more ample, so they more resembled pleasure cruisers alongside a canal than the drear Victorian mansions they mostly were. Then cut down south with a view of the new hospital across the Fulham Road at its cul, a street of altogether meaner houses, though pricily maintained and jealously lived in, as are all the West End cottages that had been purchased from the poor in the past, their pretensions jealously maintained… rows of German silver cars, all new, few pedestrians: then out onto the always refreshing passage of the Beach (the sand, the ozone).

My mobile sings.

"Where did you get to, James?"

"I fancied a walk."

"Well are you coming back?"

"Yes, in a while, I have a short rendezvous to take care of."

"Ok. See you later and we'll maybe go to John Sandoe's."

And Madeleine hangs up; and my day is open. I can remember nothing. Ground zero, day zero, zero zero.

But slowly I focus again as I pass Holmes Place and shiver at the thought of a swim and gym there – my muscles will have to remain untoned – the Delice; but I fail to be enticed by the odour of coffee and pastries issuing from its open door. The Pan bookshop almost draws me into its orbit. But I know where I am going.

Down, down, down to the place where the wells are deep with water… (the stars shone slowly in a tranquil sky, and I wondered what had become of you, and tenderly you pull my heartstrings); and I walk back down the street, and somehow feel different, although I have been here before.

But I pass her door by, letting memory suffice; for the moment.

Why?

Why am I being so obtuse with my emotions? Is it that I no longer love her, the woman behind that door? Or that I no longer trust the emotions that had bound us together for so long? Or something else… a passage of time that had subtly changed the metaphysics that lay between us; like shifting two transparent layers of a composite photograph: at first the edges and outlines of things change, a tree's leaves become smudged, a cloud elongated, a face goes out of focus; and as one continues sliding the transparencies apart every thing becomes double in the general separation; and one continues sliding them apart until nothing makes sense, unless the abstract is some kind of culmination of meaning... But this seems too glibly linear an explanation for me, and as I reach the corner of her street I fall back to wondering if in fact we cannot go back, or move forward from this black hole, to the unity we had for moments so clearly attained?

I hover on the corner. The London day suddenly has a London sky laden with cloud and a chill blows down the street, dust is blown up in flurries and I walk on up the garden square that gives onto the back of her flat.

I return under the overladen sky to the Pan bookshop.

Martin Amis; Proust; Tolkien: my eye wanders searchingly over the familiar titles. I feel at home in their ambience. A new Harry Potter shone from its multi-tiered display set up in a circular pattern by some keen assistant, a simulacrum of literary prowess squeezed into the salesman's envelope of understanding: it shone orange, red and yellow at James until he was tempted over to the table and disturbing the display by removing a copy from its stonehenge like structure, he weighed its heft in his hand, then opened the white block so two facing pages magically appeared, the weight slight, the pages oddly small, the print well spaced and separated, for children he supposed. He dipped into a line or two of text, for children also, but like Tolkien, carrying an undertow that adults could pick up – and he wondered if that's where most of the sales might be: with grown up aficionados of the fantastic?

Moving around the bookshop he picked up a volume by J.G.Ballard, "Super Cannes" it was titled, and scanning the first few pages and picking out a sentence or two to read with detailed attention, he was relieved to be back in the world of the purely adult mind, a soft frying sensation behind his forehead as half formed ideas of his own coagulated with the images flashed from the page of printed words. He replaced the paperback, sighing, deciding not to walk out with if because he did not want anything to carry in the course of his circumnavigations, but making a mental note that it was a book to purchase when opportune.

Out on the Beach the sun was making an attempt to generate some summer heat in its latest appearance between two clouds. Pleasantly warmed, his eyes dancing from the refracted sparkle and colour of objects basking in the sun's glare, James re-passed Holmes Place, and this time it invited him in for a cool swim in its dark chambers – the time was right; he dived in.

"James there you Old Rogue! Where do you think you're going? Not avoiding me again?"

"Oh! N...No."

And James turned on his heel to see the vast form of Montagu Withnail Smith baring down on him, teeth flashing, black cloak billowing out in his wake, beringed hand held aloft in a pontiff's greeting.

"Off for a swim you scallywag? Well pray delay your immersion in the holy substance for a small while it not yet being noon, the sun not having reached her zenith, and join poor Smithy, sinner that I am, in a small jar in that pleasant hostelry around the corner!" and Montagu waved his arm up out of its pontiff's pose indicating some direction over his shoulder that mostly seemed to be towards the air of heaven: then he smiled his irresistible smile, like Orson Wells as Harry Lime on the great wheel of Vienna; the same infectious drawing in to a greater and secret world one could join by simple and swift acquiescence.

So seldom being someone to resist a pleasant pressure, I nodded my assent and fell in beside my large friend as we walked the pavement, one large and one smaller, and Montagu held up a pudgy imperious hand to part the traffic as we wove through it talking amiably until we reached the other side and walked in the now plain heat down south a block to the Sporting Page, which as usual at this hour was empty, its neat pavement hogging tables shining clean under an awning. – You wait here my dear chap, while I fetch us the victuals. And without asking what I wanted Montagu dived in the invitingly open double door, and I was alone in the sun on a near silent side street, the white of the blank windowed houses glaring back at me. I sat and breathed deeply: a pause in time, a moment to re-gather.

The sun, the bleached white house walls, the sun, the rising heat from the paving stones, the tarmac, the sun bleaching the sky from blue to a mental white. A car hissed by slowly as a cat. I closed my eyes and let the sun specks swim and then putting my hands over my eyes in a childhood trick, watched the colours and patterns form: great purple sheets that glazed bright at their edges to form circles that changed from blue then to red and were whirring; then black blocks on a pale background, and speckles within the blocks that became a garden, a tree clearly etched in every detail against the bluest of summer skies – Having fun!! I took my hands away and there was Montagu baring two pints of lager, one in each hand.

" Yes, thank you.

My large friend set the drinks on the table and sat his bulk in to one of the frail chairs; he swept back his long dark hair and tossed his head so it fell decorously around his shoulders. The brooch clasping his cloak glittered; he lifted his beer and took a long heavy sip.

"The merits of a pint ere midday, while the day is yet fresh, before the sultry debris of the afternoon settles its pall of dust from the piling up of the day's events into the over-bearing afternoon; the delicate aroma of hops and the slight wizziness of drink on an empty stomach, a gurgling pleasure, a set-me-up for the trials ahead – for who knows what lies between now and that far off land and safety of bed so many hours hence?" and Withnail waved a finger. James obligingly sipped his beer to test his friend's observation. Warming to his subject: "For though we may wake pure as the lily, even as we climb out from between the white sheets the mind and body are hurtling towards the day's first commitments, even as Adam was cast from the Garden, the day is a picture of the life of man, its consummation of history and unravelling of fate, its inescapable force when a direction is taken, like a river swollen by many streams, widening and gathering pace as it nears the ocean of night, speeding up, fuller and fuller until it is no more . . . lost in the sleep of the oceans . . . "

"Quite the poet – Smith."

"What, what? yes, yes; the poet; ah ha!" And Montagu put glass to lips and a river of beer disappeared into the dark cavern of his stomach so it was an empty glass he banged down on the table. He wiped his mouth.

"Another?"

"Oh no, my boy: ample is a sufficiency to misquote somebody. I must wend my way, and you to the cleansing caverns of your baths." Montagu waited politely while James finished his beer, sipping it slowly, its taste more bitter as it warmed and lost its sparkle: he left the last quarter warm still and syrupy in its glass. Montagu was lent forward, one hand on top of another taking his weight atop the silver knobble of his cane walking stick that rose between his knees, staring pensively down the street, a slight smile playing over his features, his toes wiggling his shoes happily, the brow of his hat which he had put on against the sun, pulled down.

"Fare thee well then Montagu Withnail Smith! Are we to meet again before the closing of this day?"

"Who can know? Yet are you not calling on Madeleine again, paying your dues at the Chintz Commune, and even perhaps escorting Madeleine to the bookshop?"

"Who knows?"

And Montagu clumped James on the shoulder and sauntered off, his cloaked and hatted figure suddenly disappearing around the corner like a log swept round the corner of a raging torrent. James stared at the warm remnants of the beer he would not drink: by now Montagu would be back on the Beach.

James roused himself from the torpor the beer had induced in him, Montagu's homily on the amber nectar slightly lost to him for the moment, and hotly made his way back to Holmes Place feeling dizzy and disturbed.

But the shade of the lobby instantly reassured him and he carried his towels down to his locker. The watery ambience was thankfully deserted; the wooden lockers, the clean white tiled floor, the polished mirrors – he padded down past the easy chairs, the weighing scales, the sauna, the steam-room, and was tempted into the jacuzzi. He pressed the button and its swirling waters came to life, and finding an underwater jet he let it pummel the fatigue out of his back. A smile was spreading slowly and evenly over his face.

Then out of the jetted water and to the pool, its empty waters lapping its frescoed walls with their painted scenes of bucolic mediterranean bliss; a villa there, a vineyard there, an olive grove beneath a full moon in a sun drenched sky; lobsters and fishing boats – a scene like the pool blessed by the absence of another human form, so that James as he floated on his back in the centre of the pool, felt that he was alone in a subterranean paradise, alone in his Eden, an Adam in trunks and goggles, deaf to the world outside.

But as in all things Time grabbed him with his ugly fingers and pushed him on, and floating there he found his legs sinking and then the water was no longer holding him up and he floundered and turned so cutting a swift length through the water, and as he turned for another length a lone swimmer was climbing into his sacred pond. He hurried out for a quick sauna before changing.

In the Swedish woodland interior, ensconced in its intense heat, a small window in the door giving a passing glimpse of the outside world, the solace of one soft light completing the circle of this womb-like interior, James felt the heat finally sink into his brain so a tropical numbness overcame him and all ideas and images fled to a point where the heat and his mind were one animal, a primeval state, another point of stasis, a moment that when it was over he carried with him out of the sauna door, as one unknowingly carries seeds of deep forgotten moments throughout life to draw on like the wells they are.

When he got upstairs and out beneath the sky his phone immediately rang. It was Madeleine. Are you coming over? rather plaintively. Yes. Now? Yes. Oh good... Hermione is here.

CHAPTER TWO:
THE CHINTZ COMMUNE 12:35PM

Hermione.

There she stood in Madeleine's drawing-room, twin setish without wearing twin set, just being part of a set so stylishly was she dressed, her own set, membership of one; oddly dressed too: so obviously carefully and the clothes well chosen, demure, collected, sensitive – but her face belied it all: lonely, gaunt and with a displacement, as though she had been suffering from deep and prolonged mental anguish that disturbed her obvious beauty.

And she smiled suddenly at me so her face became what it was perhaps meant to have been: radiant and happy, the anguish that had a moment before seemed so indelibly etched in her features, gone, vanished; or was it merely good manners, her impeccable breeding, putting on the perfect front? And as she laughed and told a porky joke her demure demeanor was exposed – as a fraud? No. As a front? Closer. As another self. Correct. This bipolarism ran through and through her character like a rod: her stiff spine and elegant carriage a metaphor for the schism that lay at the heart of her confusion:

"Well, you see…", she was saying, the perfect line of her Max Mara skirt riding slightly up her smoothly and expensively stockinged leg, the fawn and dark checks against the cream background of its lightly weighted tweed nicely counterbalanced by the fresh white cotton of the blouse, the jacket almost hunting with its felt brown cuffs, all trace of drawnness gone from her now smiling and radiant face; "there was this friend of Monty's we had round at my flat for Carnival, and after he left the room to walk round in the crowds outside everyone said that he had the biggest dick in town, massive!" and she clasped her hand over mouth to cover her widening grin and she bent over slightly and shook with quiet laughter. James felt her mirth infect him, but in parallel he found he was slightly taken aback that Hermione's refinement had given way to such coarseness so seamlessly: it was almost as though she was contradicting her own character, betraying the flaws in those social graces she normally kept herself trapped inside along with her depression – the inner cause of the ravagement that showed through her features when she was not animated.

He wondered if he was alone in this assessment when he glanced over at Madeleine who was grinning broadly, drawn cleanly out of her preoccupations by Hermione's story, and clearly not seeing what I saw in Hermione. I let it pass: ". . .and so when he came back to the flat I had to know if this was true!"

Now, I had always suspected those I counted as my friends of possessing a species of measured intelligence; the kind of intelligence that is exemplified by the narrator of a novel, whom we identify with through that intelligence – a you can if not 'always trust me', at least understand and sympathize with my motives. But Hermione's sudden vulgarity and what's more Madeleine's obvious enjoyment of it caused me to feel oddly let down. Not by prudery but by the aesthetics of it. The communality 'we' who visited Madeleine's boudoir shared, was for me exemplified by a calm, call it fake if you like but maybe it was all the better for being so, a blanket of calm called into being by a retreative code of tolerant conversation – an ambient reality of reliability and ease. I wanted no frissons shivering in from the outside 'real' uncomfortable world intruding on the sensitivities of my pleasant illusion. Maybe I had it all wrong? "So I asked Monty, and he said he had seen It in the bathroom while Jim was peeing, and it was gigantic!" I was slightly revolted at the thought, that the softly spoken Jim to whom Hermione was referring might be by being so strangely endowed, cast into the realm of the purely physical: it was as though his social self which I vaguely knew had had the clothes ripped from it and beneath lay the garden slug. (Why do we find one body repellent and the next not: the one empty of form, the other godlike and perfect. Is ugliness formlessness, but beauty in the divine artist's eye, hand? And why did I find this image of Jim delivered by Hermione so wrong? And Montagu's part: was he also tarnished in my eye?). These thoughts were rushing around my head alongside others such as was I being prudish, repressed, ridiculous; and then that perhaps that I was merely tired from the exertions and heat of the streets I had been navigating. I sat down on Madeleine's floral sofa next to the small chintz covered table so covered in ornaments that there would be no room for the cup of tea I so badly craved to sit alongside them on it, if one had materialized by magic.

But for that moment I felt too fatigued to even request the beverage and lay splayed back on the sofa trying to maintain as normal a countenance as possible as the others laughed like djinns.

At that moment Montagu's large head poked through the open window.

"Anyone care to join me for lunch?"

Silence.

I felt a rustle of interest stir me. The room was hot and I felt disassociated; and although I had tasted Montagu's company once already that morning, the need for sustenance was biting into me, and I lacked the courage to begin arranging something even simple chez Madeleine's. My stirring became a movement, the raising of my head. The thought of a chill glass of white wine, the beads on the glass speckling, the lemonish, butter taste pricking my appetite and reviving my senses, floated before my mind's eye; a pleasant dish before me, the bread broken; and after all I could happily bear Montagu for the duration.

He caught my subtle movement: Ah, James will come. Anyone else? But there were no takers, the girls still wrapped in a feminine bubble of giggles, subdued now, secret even from the betrayer of the initial confidence whose head haloed by sunlit sparkling black curls leant so confidently through the window. Montagu smiled encouragingly at me; and I fought the inertia that had seized my body and mind and raised myself to standing, head spinning slightly still, mind gently focusing on the anticipated pleasure ahead. I mumbled my goodbyes thankfully not needing to explain this time why or where I was going since it was obvious, and stumbled along the darkened lobby and hallway leading out of Madeleine's house, then found myself walking in the sun-drenched street alongside Montagu, keeping up with his rapid, long strides.

We crossed the busy north running feeder road, the counterpart of the south running Redcliffe Gardens one walked down on the way to the Beach, the endless stream of cars and vans washing north along a narrower thoroughfare of altogether meaner houses and scant trees. Across the other side up against the cemetery was our rendezvous in a small corner of streets of snug local bars and restaurants, caught as it was between larger no mans lands of the type that make London so deeply alienating, a counterpart to its polite regions – rather the same dichotomy as I had observed in Hermione's character: I chuckled aloud but to myself at the elaborate analogy I had constructed; Montagu cast me a slightly suspicious look; but just then the phone rang.

It was Her.

So little communication and now this. My heart warmed, which I surmised meant something, something positive. Hello, in a singsong voice on a sweet high pitch she greeted me. My feet strummed the pavement as I followed Montagu on. I haloed back but my voice sounded husky to me, empty of emotion. Not that I was, not that I was. Speaking to her now, hearing her voice, I felt better, much improved, as though my mind had switched from a congealed tangle of raw wires to a well structured transistor. I told her I was in the area. I didn't tell her I had passed by her door and contemplated us, nor that I was about to eat with Montagu – I had barely enough money to eat out myself let alone invite my hungry loved one with her insatiable appetites. I said cheerfully, almost manfully, that I would call in an hour's time, determining to do so as I noted the time: 12:57, and folded the phone. Montagu fell back into step with me as we came into sight of the awning of the restaurant. He wiped his brow appearing petulant or somehow discomfited.

For some reason they would only seat us downstairs, so down the spiral staircase we went and the head chef who came out to meet Montagu was welcoming and effusive but in a laid back way; Montagu lapped it up, and seated himself against the cream coloured wall on the banquette, squeezing his bulk past the table that the waiter pushed back over his lap with a smile: A bottle of your Alsace, he barked, not looking at the waiter, picking up a knife and inspecting it. The wine arrived promptly and it had an immaculately dry but fruity taste which is the way only expensively made wines are constructed. Fine wine, I said, and proceeded to relate Hermione's little fable concerning Jim's dick. I don't know why I did so: Montagu was already in a heavy mood by the feel and looks of things, and no doubt he knew what he had himself manufactured in Hermione's flat the August before; and no doubt also there would be inconsistencies in Hermione's relating of the incident which might wind Montagu up – or it could have all been a darn right lie, a fabrication by her, though James doubted this latter as not in keeping with Hermione's character, although remembered he had just discounted the veracity of his knowledge her character. He felt himself altogether on the short end of a losing game, but somehow Monty's bad mood had encouraged him and now the words were out.

Montagu purpled. He gulped half a glass of expensive Alsace, and looked at me.

"Why did you repeat that to me?" he asked in a dangerously acid tone. I had just been asking myself the same question; and the conjectures, half formulated that I had come out with would scarcely bare the test of repetition. My hesitation seemed to irk him. So deciding honesty was the best tactic I replied: I don't know.

It wasn't.

Montagu drained his glass, thumped it down on the table and refilled it. "I've no means of paying for this meal," he announced as the waiter thrust menus into our hands. The prices were very high I noticed from a cursory glance. I was beginning to feel uncomfortable. Some little starters we hadn't ordered arrived; chef's offerings. – Yes you do, he said, popping a mille-feuille covered delicacy between his rose bud lips. – I don't follow you? – Well you followed her closely enough. – But I found the whole story distasteful! – Exactly, that's why you repeated it! – What's it to you anyway? I asked, nibbling a small corner of one of the tiny delicacies, my appetite wholly vanished.

"What's it to me? he asks! Just that my name is being bandied about willy nilly by a bunch of half brained nincompoops! Just that my reputation in being dragged though the drawing rooms of Chelsea, just that I have never fancied Jim–"

"I have never objected to your homosexuality!" I interrupted. A slight sweat was making my collar swim, and a worrying heat was rising into my face.

"Some of your best friends…" Monty spat across the table linen at me.

I rose to leave.

"I will not pay for your lunch nor countenance that remark; I was merely relating a slightly stupid story of Hermione's in which your name came up!"

"Oh, sit down, sit down; for Christ's sake can't you grow up James! Can't you see that I'm just a bit moody; hot and hungry, that's what it is. Don't concern yourself with paying. Be my guest," he said.

I sat down with a thump: "but how will you pay if you have no money?"

"I will simply tell the manager at the end of the meal that I have none, and give him my name and address. If he makes a fuss I shall tell him that he may call the police, and that I shall furnish them with my name and address, which I am sure they know already!"

"And they won't arrest you?"

"Why, no! Of course not! Don't be absurd!" said the indefatigable Montagu. He refilled his own glass and topped up mine and replaced the empty bottle of Alsace upside down in the ice bucket. Another! he called as he took a large sip.

"Well, was it big? Enormous?" I asked my friend as I placed my hands fifteen inches apart palms facing; then I nimbly sipped the honeyed wine.

And we both burst out into long fits of hysterical laughter, that subsided so slowly that they lasted us the whole meal.

Meantime my appetite had transformed back from vanished to famished.

◆ ◆ ◆ ◆ ◆ ◆

A long bubbly mirth. An inner sanctum of smile rolling over irritation, depression, the dark side kept so tremulously out: out of this here and now in this merry basement, its air conditioning cooling the soft electric glow of the light bulbs, the stone floors cool to the feet, the fine food gracing the senses, delicately pulling them alive – and yet, into my mind kept flashing other thoughts more disturbing, more mundane: I should call her, when? The figure 12:57 burned against the dark screen of my mind glowing as they did on my phone, and I was mentally adding one hour: 13:57, then translating it into English: three minutes to two; that meant to all intents and purposes two o'clock, a time I could file away for instant and easy recall; but how long 'til two. I pulled my phone from my pocket as Monty was spinning into another yarn, about Jim of all things: had the man forgotten the impasse between us caused by his supposed faux pas just recounted by Hermione, or was he being merely obtuse? I shrugged inwardly, 13:29; so half an hour to go, though I didn't have to be precise; after all it was only a call to my – but I had to wrench my attention back to our lunchtime banter, as it had become, and pay attention to Montagu as he was reaching his punchline in the latest Jim story, and he demanded it: "…so he said the wine was too expensive so I slapped him. What a disastrous evening!" And although I had missed the beginning of the story so immersed had I been in placing my future in time, a strong image of Montagu sitting next to Jim on the banquette petulantly slapping his cheek in that offensive but otherwise meaningless way I could so easily imagine of him, one so well mannered and kind, although driven to distraction by the near constantly weak state of his nervous system – a simulacrum of a childish strike but delivered by a grown man, overgrown in height and girth, painless but ill tempered; or did such poses turn him on. I changed the track of the subject looming in my mind not wanting to enquire any more deeply into such tendencies in my friend. Let them be hidden from me, and as I avert my gaze perhaps they are not happening, those strange privacies of another's life that I am not privy to, and neither want to be.

And what I liked, appreciated about Montagu, is that he was sensitive to my delicacy on this as on so many other issues, and did not push in any direction that was not wanted (Except when very drunk when he could become obnoxious, as he obviously had been with Jim.) And then it occurred to me that perhaps there was more to him and Jim, that they were emotionally entangled, even physically, sometimes. I wondered at Montagu, and where his inability to find a partner was leading him – but further conjecture was cut by the arrival of yet another dish. This was going to be a pricey repast.

Now. Seeing Myself. Thinking of her. And all the women of my life drift past as in the temptation of Saint Anthony: their forms beseeching the praying monk of the wilderness to turn his eyes from God and feast on them instead. Which the greater illusion?

I itch for Withnail to finish: this lunch, this conversation – I feel the need to be away and reinvent myself. I don't like this atmosphere any more!

I see the faces of my lovers pass me, melt one into another; as Withnail speaks on, slurping coffee into his wondrous rosebud mouth.... as a parade; they melt one face into the next like the women in Albert Camus' l'Étranger: the archetypical woman – and James remembers when making love to Trisha how her face became Cynthia's, became Leila's; the face of the female goddess: matter transformed into pure form; by? by...? His brain fused, emblazoned by disappearing images trailing across the dark night of his unconscious. He reached, as though through a wall of a dream/sleep, for the wine and sipped its Alsatian nectar; and again; and felt marginally reenergized.

Monty was peering at him oddly – as an owl might peer – at its victim?

"Shall we go?" mumbled James.

"I'll call for the bill."

"The Old Bill; you mean?"

Montagu laughed a short bitter sound and clicked his fingers. After a wait that felt as tedious as that in a dentist's waiting room, the sad finale to so many a fine meal (wasn't there a better way – like having the bill sent to your home – like a parking ticket), the sheet of innocent white paper arrived. Montagu looked at me – sorrowfully almost;

I sighed and picked it up. I shall not repeat the sum to my dear reader, neither wishing to shock them nor to draw their attention away from the central plot, which is not, I repeat not about money!

I let the absurdist line of women somnambulate through my mind again, as I fiddled with a credit card – I did not after all wish Montagu Withnail Smith esq. to end up in an embarrassing posture, in his own manor too.

He began beaming as he realized I was in fact paying; a spreading beam like the sun on a fine Suffolk summer's morn. I was happy he was happy. My wallet was not: as the crypto-fascists who now rule Italy are described as anti anti-fascists, the same negative logical chain applied to my mood – not good! So I let the ladies parade out again, walking, following each other off stage right, into the wings so to speak .

…I waved Monty off at the entrance/exit and unfolded my mobile as he strode away, my happy friend and his bulbous body, tapping cane, billowing cloak, flowing away from me in a haze of good food and drink. Reborn bonhomie.

It was the beautiful Silvanna croaking her mornings (for her a late riser) into my ear. As her moanings began to gather pace, and I knew there would be a long period of this before she got round to mentioning what cocktail party or soirée she was going to invite me to attend with her, and since my mind was poised to jump into conversation with Victoria (Her); I casually asked the dear Silvanna to call me later as I was 'in the middle of something', my latest variant of the put-off remark.

♦ ♦ ♦ ♦ ♦ ♦

"I'm so depressed," she said: "I can't do anything about it. My lack of money caused my depression but now I am de-

31

pressed I can't function, can't do anything, especially chasing money." – crossing my mind was the credit card slip I had just signed – it would only have been a blip on the horizon of what she needed – perhaps I should buy a lottery ticket? At least one chance in a million for a million is better than none.

A gentle wind ruffled through my hair and a splash of sunshine warmed my skin, arm hairs glowing gold against tan, watch glinting like a shark. Across the road was the shadowy interior of a Paki newsagent. I told Viki I would call straight back and folding the phone went into the shade of the shop.

Instantly my eyes adjusted to the motley selection of magazines, cigarettes and chocolate bars. I put one pound on the counter: "Lucky dip please." A ticket spewed out of the machine; he balding in a white nylon button shirt, passed me my ticket efficiently. I folded it into my wallet without looking at the numbers I had drawn. The playoff would be on the morrow.

Back outside – the white houses of Ifield Road blinding in the sun, the pale white of an English summer's day (not the yellowish white of the South). The black tarmac, the grey pavement and the sky whiting over now – a study in two-tone, and I felt for the moment as though I was walking across the set of a sixties film: David Hemmings, or Colin MacInnes – City of Spades, and I was the absolute beginner.

But of course I was not. And the illusion was broken by the passage down the street and past my feet of one of those louche post-modern gin palaces packed with electronics that pass as the contemporary car. It was driven by a diminutive lady; I felt an upsurge of anger at the beast, as much for disturbing my reverie of time displacement as for the wanton consumer horror of overdoneness represented by this zooshing two tons of German metal… and I was no more a beginner than the oldest of great tortoises – absolute maybe – but only in the sense that I knew too much – had seen too much; and nowadays I did too little.

I sauntered up the street allowing snippets of the black and white film-set illusion to re-invade my consciousness, in a pleasant inconsequential way.

Was I moving towards the enchanted apartment of Madeleine – or the deprived excesses and emotional feast of Victoria.

For, what was my commitment to her? Did the C word have a nature, a describable basis; or was it merely an emotion, to be analyzed the way one's emotions run? Commitment. A solid word: but in practice so amorphous. I shook my head. And to which face in the gallery of my loves should I focus on: the Archetype? The Amalgam? The perfection? The Goddess? – or just the imperfect, depressed mortal on the end of the phone who embodied all of the above; and none of it.

This soliloquy on love… but why call it love – why not call it falling for the archetype? Reaching to the other? Finding the self or, I just give wriggle and split down the middle ~ then there are two of me. Is that what love is? The wish for there to be two of me?

I kick a can idly with my foot. It clutters loudly into the street in a way that disturbed the air and made me realize how quiet it had been. A woman looked up from her clipping of a diminutive hedge across the road, and then she took in my appearance and looked confused: I guess that so well dressed a man should be so loutish in his behaviour.

Well dressed?

But I wasn't really – not suited or tied; I rarely was – but well fitted if you like, tailored almost, but not – expensively in a fashion, but again not really – dressing is the art of forgetting what you are wearing – and that can change during the course of a day; with moods. I looked down at my boots: Chelsea boots fittingly – they were rather nice. But my trousers depressed me as trousers do – not a pretty garment, trousers: men don't look so much better when wearing tights or skirts though they are more comfortable. I found myself vainly hoping that fashion might change enough in my lifetime to allow me the latitude to adopt what was for now considered feminine costume: was society really so macho? I supposed it was.

I stared at the can, crashed into the gutter between two cars in the dust on the far side of the road.

♦ ♦ ♦ ♦ ♦ ♦

…"the far side of the road" – the Van the Man riff echoed in my inner ear as I walked, veering away from Madeleine's, towards Viki's.

On the far side of the road is exactly where I felt I stood.

♦ ♦ ♦ ♦ ♦ ♦

But as I was taking the corner into Redcliffe Gardens who should approach but Dulcie Sassoon!

She looked madly drunk as she peered at me widely as through a screen, bad-hair-day wisps that she was petulantly brushing back as though her large hair was conspiring against her rather than she against it. Yet she was not as drunk as she appeared which could be ascertained from her amble, which in fact was normal enough, for her.

"Where are you going?" she asked without preamble, though we had not bumped into each other for a few weeks.

"Dunno," I sort of lied.

"I'm going to Madeleine's. Do you think Monty is there?"

"Could be. Just had lunch with him."

"That must have been expensive for you."

Warmed by her perspicacity I smiled. So did she. We laughed.

"Come on then," I said gamely, "I'll walk with you there."

James

CHAPTER THREE:
INSIDE THE CHINTZ COMMUNE 2:01PM

"I'm not sure Montagu's talking to me though," Dulcie said nervously. "Do you think I should go?"

"You are on your way there, so yes!"

"But I'm afraid he will still be angry with me: you see, we all went to Ballams, and I spose I mixed my medication with a drink or two, so hard not to, my bloody mother, won't help, all the money's gone to my brother, bloody bitch. So we went to Ballams and Theo Lansdowne was there and Mo, and I did lose it, threw a glass at the window, told Monty to fuck off; think I've been banned. Perhaps I shouldn't go in with you?" Theo Lansdowne's face swam before my inner eye. I could imagine him there in Ballams sitting opposite Mo, Mohamed Mogul that is, the restaurateur, a look of fake shocked horror pouting out of his small round mouth above his Edwardian white beard, his piggy eyes screwing up in his round red face, and Mo used to restaurant brawls because he owned several, quietly taking everything in, swaying in his eastern way, showing nothing but his smile.

Exasperating Dulcie Sassoon, always making her mental state the centre of the universe. "He will have forgotten about it; come on!" I commanded. She followed obediently. But there was another rebellion on the steps as I was pressing Madeleine's bell.

"Goodbye!"

The buzzer went to let us in. "But what makes you think he is still angry with you?"

"I did call him a fucker."

"That's not so bad."

She looked at her shoes: other worse observations on Montagu's character had obviously been aimed by her at him. Perhaps that was why he had been peeved at the start of our lunch?

"Oh. Goodbye!" I waved cheerfully. That did it.

"Okay. I'm coming in then!" Dulcie heaved a deep breath and climbed her short rotund self up the steps… we were pacing the soft carpet of the familiar dark hallway, and then the small lobby.

"Is that you?" Madeleine was calling.

It obviously was: whoever you was, was us.

Oh Madeleine. Madeleine – stretched out like the African Queen, dreaming of your servants in the 'ol South, surrounded by your courtiers.

Hermione was still there- a tell tale bottle of white wine stood nearly empty on the narrow buffet table that stretched thin along the back wall of the drawing-room next to the open doorway. She looked more melted than usual, the gaunt lines

of her face melted by insobriety, her carefully worn clothes
rucked up slightly – she looked, oh so human!

And Montagu was there, a large figure, a silhouette
framed by the kitchen window at the far end of the corridor,
moving about jauntily.

"Montagu is preparing something for us to eat," Madeleine
chirped. "Are you hungry?"

"Whya neeow," I parodied Madeleine's Southern drawl.
"We'orl juss ate, Monty and I."

"… Well if you're not hungry. And what about you Dulcie?" asked Madeleine as Ms Sassoon stumbled out of the
dimness of the corridor and into the brightly blazed afternoon
sunlit front room.

"You what?" she stumbled around, obviously blinded.
"Oh hello Hermione," she blinked. "Food? Oh no. Perhaps a
little. Mustn't drink, must I? But a little glass of wine… "

"There's none left. You can always go out and buy us a
bottle," Madeleine said down her nose not particularly liking
Dulcie at that moment, and thinking, as she had to, of her
purse and her own need.

"Oh!" exclaimed Dulcie, eyeing the remnants of the
sancerre on the thin sideboard. I felt I had performed my pe-
cuniary duty at lunch and felt no immediate urge to volunteer
my finances.

It was generally credited that Dulcie Sassoon was fabu-
lously rich; or rather that her family was – but they had rather
cast her aside, financially at any rate, as through the seventies
she had performed her Marianne Faithful impersonation and
wrecked herself on the wheel of sex, drugs and rock an' roll
– which accounted for the shape she was in now! rotund with
a placid sag to her overeager features; a body which perhaps
still refused to believe it wasn't in its first flight of youth. But
still the myth of money persisted around her, an aura that

clung like old scent: thus Madeleine's unspoken aside – rich Dulcie could buy the booze. Yet, and this was no doubt the truth, she was not rich. The wealthy denizens that inhabited the state rooms of her family homes were eeking her out on a meagre allowance so as to prevent her return to her errant ways and curtail her current drinking. In their dreams.

Interrupting this surmise of mine buzzed the front door bell. In was let a disheveled character in worn clothes that looked stylish despite themselves, balding hair that might once have been brownish and a baby face dominated by lips of bulbous sensitivity and wild eyes that darted about the room blindly. Yet when he opened his mouth he was as softly spoken as they come, his dulcet tones telling of a beguiling wit and sophistication.

"Jerry Rafael," he introduced himself to me very properly. I shook the proffered limp hand:

"James Low."

"We've met before," he dropped his head as he spoke and looked at me as a wildebeest might if it was about to be shot. We had not. Definitely.

"I don't think so," I answered so as not to seem peremptory.

"The Saddle Room; some woman with a French name."

"Never been there. Before my time."

"Oh? Could have sworn!" and a mischievous play animated his face: he wasn't going to allow his little game to come between him and a new acquaintance.

I smiled back, genuinely liking him. And maintaining his broken grin he produced from the hallway where he had no doubt deposited it on his furtive entrance a guitar, very old broke and stained.

"Can I play you my new song? he addressed no one in particular. "Can the wordless and those who give no voice to thought be truly human, or are they half dead?" he demanded vehemently turning on Dulcie who had taken advantage of the attention drawn to his antics to surreptitiously pour herself the remainder of the sancerre.

"What on earth are you talking about?" she answered haughtily, staring down at Jerry clutching his guitar if she could have from her short stature.

"Where'd you get that wine?" Jerry Rafael snapped back. I admired the wilyness apparent in this answer, as though he had somehow known or guessed at Madeleine's failure to offer Dulcie a drink and Dulcie's failure to buy a new bottle, and the likelihood he would have to remain dry too.

"Shall I play to you then?"

"Yes," drawled Madeleine, taking his invitation as her due.

"All right;" and he sat on the floor right there in the open place before the fire in his filthy tweed jacket and began strumming some dreadfully dissonant out of tune chords that remained strangely musical.

"Can't remember that one," he intoned.

Montagu's head appeared at the door attracted by the chords: "Why! If music be the food of love, play on, for I have prepared us a wonderful repast – yes I know we have just eaten but this is for those others less fortunate," he said in an aside to me. "This calls for wine! Let me pop out and acquire us a drink!" and he ruffled a wad of readies between his fingers as though he was a conjuror at a show.

You old rascal, I thought.

◆ ◆ ◆ ◆ ◆ ◆

The door slammed on Montagu Withnail Smith who had departed in a flurry of loud words and swirling cloak.

Jerry was sitting on the carpet, and he re-pitched his tuneless tune, and magically it turned into a song, quite a witty one, lyrical and succinct:

"Oh my God, if there really is one..."

it began, and was song in a cockney two-time. But then he stumbled, his fingers entangled in the strings like a catatonic struggling with a broken cat's cradle, a lost look glazing his eyes. Jerry laid the guitar down again. It was difficult to believe him capable of the rendition of a complete song – but obviously he could: I could see his 'collected' songs CD with his picture on its cover which had spilt out of his duffle bag onto the carpet. The photo of him was of a vastly more dapper person than the sprite sitting in front of us now... there was something about him, an aura; he had definitely been or was somebody. But who, he probably no longer even knew himself.

The doorbell rang again and I was expecting Withnail Smith's return, so was surprised when the figure who walked into the room with his arms outstretched calling out hello, hello, like an insecure prima donna, was that of Theo Lansdowne, the playwright.

His arms still apart he rushed on his small feet over to Madeleine and air kissed her so she did not have to touch his white Edwardian style goatee or red corpuscular cheeks; then he turned on the thin Hermione who almost fell back at the breath of his coming. Then there was me, whom he was content to shake by the hand, vigorously, "James, James, so GOOD to see you," and he managed a follow up chortle then collapsed into a chair as though all these introductory exertions had exhausted him, his hugely rotund belly forcing him almost to lie rather than sit. Hermione looked like a waif standing hesitantly in the middle of the room, searching for a side to place her now empty glass on. She chose the mantelpiece. Chink. She set it down. The flames of the fire licked idly orange and gold. The room was too hot. I walked to the large central window of the bay and opened its lower half all the way up so it doubled with its mirror glass above. It opened to just above my hair line. Outside the street was sultry warm. Nothing was going on but the green leaves on the trees blowing softly in the air currents. A small bent man carrying a heavy box walked into my view, followed by a large upright figure goading him , some paces behind which resolved itself of a sudden in my vision into Montagu. He came into the room followed by the shopkeeper who was carrying the large box. "Here sa?" "Yes, fine. Thank you." The shopkeeper left. When I peered into the box it contained twenty-four bottles of Italian beer, four bottles of Grand Echezaux and a magnum of Krug.

It was going to be one of those days.

Montagu received an air brush kissing from Theo Lansdowne, accepting his beard with grace: two queens performing their ritual dance. Theo turned on Dulcie a mock look of friendship neatly composed on his lips, only his mocking eyes giving him away: "Recovered from Ballams?" he uttered innocently.

For a moment the weakness inherent in Dulcie's character showed through as she hesitated between violent reaction and ignoring Theo's provocative reminder of her faux pas. Her face changed colour from red to white several times as everybody watched her. "I presume they have got the wine stains out of the curtains!" Theo followed up with a wry and not very convincing little chortle. But he had overstepped.

"Oh come off it Theo!" barked Montagu, a huge unamusedness biting the atmosphere in the room. Theo's jaw clamped shut like a reprimanded servant's, and Dulcie, let off the hook, rescued even, by the man she had insulted at Ballams relaxed into a warm thankfulness and positively beamed at Montagu. Friends again, I muttered to myself.

Not so Theo, who had transferred his venom to Montagu with a long look of spite. But no one paid Theo any attention least of all Montagu as the Krug was popped and the afternoon sun streamed in through the far side of the bay lighting up the particles of dust in the room in a soporific haze; and the atmosphere in the room seemed to shift on into another time: the fire crackled and conversation leapt, and even Theo was mollified.

I was sitting by the fire in one of the Empire chairs which was upright enough to keep one alert while comfortable enough to relax one; a perfect chair no less: so typical of Madeleine's discreet intelligence to place it where it was.

The drink was flowing. Outside the day had darkened again until the gloom coming through the window represented night more than day; I blessed the English weather and its changeability. I felt I might sit where I was forever as I cradled a glass of the fine red burgundy, and watch the people in the room as they postured around like fish in an aquarium, unmolested by any advances by any of them as I was – protected inside some mystical auric bubble which they must sense. Montagu and Dulcie were enjoying a flirtatious banter; Theo Lansdowne was sat like I was observing, perhaps divining lines for his next play; Madeleine was chatting amiably with Hermione while Jerry the guitar was trying vainly to join in: the two women were ignoring his mumbled occasional interruptions.

The wine, the fire, the gloom outside and the warmth and colour inside – all conspired to let steal over me a rug of contentment. I stretched my legs out and crossed my finely booted feet over. The wine felt like a rich torrent of royal purples and gold, reflected in its majestic cost; and it was wonderfully hallucinogenic.

So, it was time to move on. Enough of this stupor, stupidity, diverting as it was. And was not the fineness of the wine somewhat wasted on this crowd? I should take its lingering power elsewhere.

James

CHAPTER FOUR:
THE LOST HOUR 2:28PM

Through the top floor window of the modern hospital west London lay resplendent under a now bright sunlit blue sky. James breathed deeply as he looked out at the scene as fresh as an alpine winter under snow. Beneath, six deep floors down, the beach wove its usual busy way east and west, to and fro, the tops of buses like red toys as they inched along.

The buzzer buzzed, slightly startling him, and he turned to see the nurse gesture to him impatiently to pass on through the cordon sanitaire and enter the hermetically sealed corridor leading to intensive care.

On entering into the sanctum he washed his hands in a medical solution, donned rubber gloves, plastic shoe covers and a hair net, and was led down the long corridor by a friendly sister who seemed intelligent and relaxed as though she had stepped out of an altogether calmer less capitalist era. He peered out at the same view as they walked, but now it lacked resonance and proximity, its panorama of a gilded city wholly artificial compared with the immediacy of the plastic floor they padded down.

Turning a corner, a row of beds, bodies like meat at the butchers, hacked and red, bones and innards on full display. They passed without comment.

And there, all alone in an isolated room, the view behind his immobile head so he could never see it, lay Troy, his body broken by misuse, his mind clouded by the morphine they filled him with to dull the pain: the same pain he had sought for so long to escape by throwing himself into the abuses that had rendered him so low down.

"So wonderful to see you; so nice; so wonderful!" came the familiar singsong voice issuing from between the tubes and bandages – and a pair of black stoned eyes found James and weakly glued themselves to his, searching for warmth – meaning they had stopped looking for.

At least that battle is over, thought James. For so long Troy had failed to fight the demons finally unleashed by his mother's death. He simply refused to get over it, and with his ample inheritance from her had thrown himself into a life of drunken orgy, hoping perhaps that the winds of substance abuse would clear his mind as though by remote; believing possibly that there really is no price to be paid – but the price was here, too terrible and shocking to contemplate as the grim reaper hovered to collect his morbid dues. Perhaps this planet is too old and steeped in sickness ever to overcome the evil inherent in life, James conjectured miserably in an unusually pessimistic frame – and a whole vision unfurled to him of a continuum of history stretching back from now as full of horror and uncertainty as the present moment; empires rose and fell before his minds eye; peoples slaughtered each other; fathers raped daughters; mothers disowned sons and nature conspired in her indifference until the whole sorry ship became infested with an ever growing malice and affliction... . his desperate reverie was broken by a familiar voice, warm to his ear, and a thrill as a friendly and familiar hand closed gently on his arm. "My God; it's shocking!" she said, and planted a kiss on my cheek. "Gwen," I whispered in a soft voice, as though breathing life into a ghost.

"James!" she looked at me all blank, her worker's hand, so out of place in one so delicate, still resting on my arm like a small bird perched sheltering in a tree. "Let's go and get coffee," she said, the warmth of her voice still showing through her stunned look.

We walked out of the hospital and across the Beach and along it towards the cinema. Gwen walked on her long legs in her elegant way, head held high without her nose going up, her eyes darting around as though constantly searching for something: but when they met mine they were all warmth and that smile enlivened her good looks – as though she were leading one on into a hidden playground of forbidden treasures. It felt good to be beside her.

Images of Troy flashed through my mind, prone on his bed like a wounded baby. We sat down at the pub table; no coffee then. Vodka tonic it was: some things never change... always the bon viveur with that extra mile and style – all that Hermione possessed but so much more, and that surety of nose that invariably led her to the richest pickings – perhaps her success as a bond trader had taught her some arcane laws of some jungle and it helped her? anyhow, she seemed, on the surface, to have relegated Troy and his predicament to a bottom drawer, so pragmatic was her instinct for survival, her vulnerability not to be compromised in this instance, or any other no doubt.

So much he read into her face in a few instants, so it was with a slight vacuous sensation that he faced her across the table, half pint in hand. It needn't have bothered him. Her phone chirruped mercilessly and she was leaping up and pacing as she talked six to the dozen to the hidden caller; then lurched outdoors for a quick puff; then bumping into someone she knew and conducting a shouted conversation in sloaney codes so even the roar of the traffic was dimmed. She came back in and gave James some face time: for about twenty seconds. How shocking Troy is; what a waste; all that booze, white powder, all night parties, gay encounters; all that money; gone! Then she was stopped, her mobile calling her away to the wireless world, a virtual world where nothing really mattered, and one's own hand in encouraging the disaster on the sixth floor across the road was scarcely recognized: not that there was anything one could do; anything. James played this fictitious monologue in his head as though it was real while Gwendolin again marched up and down the other side of the pub windows, yakking into her mobile her other hand pirouetting a cigarette in a mad dance that sometimes reached her lips. He wondered if he was not being unfair, that she was not thinking this way, and was simply as shocked as he was. He just didn't know.

She came back in – her car was on the double yellow; must rush; next week? and she was gone in a billow of clothes and there was only an empty place where she had been, her full on energy now rendered as virtual as her being. James sat on alone for a moment as though stunned; then gathered himself up and forced himself out into the sunlit street. He felt the rays revive him somewhat. I need a break, some peace, some insight, he thought.

Seen from the sixth floor of the hospital above he appeared a small figure standing slightly hunched that turned one way and then the other without walking on, then stared at the sky, then of a sudden hailed a cab and climbing in the cab moved off soon lost in the ongoing weave of traffic. The watcher might have conjectured as to what he had been up to; but he never would have known.

James

CHAPTER FIVE:
THE MEDITATION 3:07PM

James entered through the painted white door that was not locked and creaked on its hinges, swinging back closed behind him and with a soft thud shutting out the street behind him as he trod forward on the coir matting that carpeted the airy corridor ahead and spread its browness into large, light, glaring white high ceilinged rooms he could glance into as he advanced past their swing doors that were propped open to either side of him; empty white painted rooms, their large Victorian windows facing out onto nondescript views of whitewashed walls, flowering buddleias waving their butterfly fronds in the breeze, and the quiet backs of other houses. The rooms' ceiling flowers and cornices so overpainted with layer over layer of white that all detail had disappeared into a general indifference: a rose had become a two dimensional blob – a relief pattern lost to geometric understanding – the indifference of these buddhists to their surroundings was so selective.

Yet here he was, monastically retreating rather than getting drunk at the Chintz Commune, or trying to keep up with Gwen after their visit to Troy.

A mousy girl approached him an official look of enquiry knitting her brow.

"I've come for the 3:30 meditation," James explained in what he hoped was a soft tone; though it sounded too unctuous to his ear as unfamiliar dulcet tones issued out of his mouth.

She glanced at her neat silver finish wrist watch (only should a buddhist be so time oriented and wear such a glittering artifact?). "You'd better hurry. They're starting now and you can't go in after they have started. (Yes I can and shut up both sprang to mind). She moved off.

"But where is the class?"

"Room six!" she answered crossly, still moving away. We didn't like each other.

Where's that , I was going to ask, but gave up on her. I climbed some stairs – from the landing there was a view of some gardens below and a busy street with a bar with a large pavement café in front of it. People were sitting idly at the tables in the sun, their warming beer losing its fizz and their cappuccinos losing froth – the afternoon was turning sultry.

As I climbed up to the corridor which ran directly above the one below I saw people through a half open door; I went up to it. A bearded man was talking to a small group sat on the floor of another coir matted over-white room; the ceilings though were lower here on the first floor lessening the impact.

"Meditation?" My voice sounded better this time: gruff, sincere, masculine. The bearded man looked up at me and smiled: come on in.

I sat in an empty space at the side near one of the three large Victorian windows that framed the room. By the time I had tuned into what the bearded man was saying he had finished his preamble, and was giving instructions on the meditation we were to do – instructions most had heard before it seemed, for they were succinct to the point of brevity.

Watch your breath as it comes in and as it goes out. Scan your attention through your body. These are the two techniques we shall be using today: the beard smiled and surveyed his class turning his head.

I closed my eyes and concentrated on my breathing. After a while I scanned up and down my body, trying to concentrate. But inevitably my eyes would flutter open or an extraneous thought would creep in: I closed my eyes again and let the thought move on.

Flashes! Flashes of thought through my closed eyes: I was in Madeleine's front room; I saw the photograph of a car; I was perusing the same photograph, holding the magazine, sitting in a room I had never visited apart from in present imagination. I allowed the picture to vanish. I was back in the meditation room. My leg ached so I stretched it out. Slowly the ache dissipated; I left it and remembered to concentrate, on breath, and listened and felt as my lungs filled and emptied and I felt the wind of my breath in my nostrils. My eyes opened. Light was streaming in through the large window above my right shoulder. I closed my eyes and my optic nerve swam with blinding light for a moment. I shifted my attention to my body; felt the whole tingle, vibrate harmoniously, and a sudden feeling of intense well being and uplift coursed through me as though I had just woken up for the first time that day. And the voice of the old masters came to me: 'be not attached to good feelings or bad feelings; just observe them." And then, still feeling floatingly fantastic I recalled to myself the motto Bruce Lee had inscribed on the back of the medallion he wore, the one he was wearing when he died:

using no way as way
having no limitation as limitation
… And I close my eyes again.

In my mind's eye I see swimming white pools left by the light from the windows of the room on my inner retina; shapes coagulate and change, vortexes, cubes, followed by stabs of floating colour – and then I smile gently to myself for I understand that it is my imagination that is in control of the images and that I am not simply passively observing them – so I play with the shapes and colours and soon discover that sometimes I can change them but other times they change of their own volition, or what seems like it. After a while I see a white light only, pure and radiant as though bathing my vision; the while light intensifies, intensifies and intensifies, until almost I believe it is blinding me and in a surge of panic I almost break the trance by opening my eyes! But instead I deepen my breathing and relax. But the light gets brighter still so I feed in some colour from my imagination and soon the white light is flecked with swirling pools of blue like a painted neon strip. Thoughts arise: I think of my cat and see her face whirring towards me as though on a 3-D projection screen! She bares her teeth and hisses. I raise a hand and duck–

"Anything the matter! says the instructor, breaking me out of the… the… the er what? I must have looked very strange for him to have broken the session. I nodded a weak yes and sat on as the room returned to meditative silence and the teacher's eye shifted back to his concentration. But I only stared up at the window with its large sky flowing slowly.

I stood up and carefully walked out of the meditation room. The bearded teacher glanced up, shocked.

Out on the corridor, near the landing he caught up with me. He was a bit breathless and ruffled.

"Are you leaving?"

"Yup."

"You can't leave in the middle of a meditation!"

"Yes I can."

"It could be terribly dangerous!"

"Be water, my friend," I uttered as enigmatically as I could.

He stood there mouth agape, beard wagging. A bead of sweat appeared on his brow.

Smiling gently I left him clutching the banister staring after me as I climbed down the stairs and was lost to him in the sudden dimness of the lower corridor.

There I passed the mousy girl. She was carrying a clipboard. I kept my smile; but it was not for her: I felt genuinely happy – I had enjoyed my space of introspection – and I was happy that she did not accost me further. And I opened the front door which offered me a goodbye creak as I stepped out into the golden sun-drenched afternoon sun, and thought – how good to be free, free to be on this street when I please, and, and to chase a beer at that very colourful looking pavement café with those oh so indolent citizens.

I crossed the hot street and at the wooden counter inside in the cool shade asked for a beer. It came cold in the glass. I let it stand and watched the glass break into necklaces of beads then slowly raised it to my lips and allowed the rush of cold liquid slake my thirst and send a bubble of pleasure to my brain where it exploded gently and the sun outside picked out the outlines of people just perfectly; and my pleasure was added to by the illicitness of no longer being in that sultry meditation centre any longer. And I thought of the bearded man and his class still there as I drank, and the mousy woman, and thought how much more pure pleasure than they I was achieving.

Life is for action, I resolved, not for introspection: that I can achieve after I am dead. Yet, as I looked off towards Portobello and Notting Hill Gate I felt an empty space there where I had had my eyes closed – and in that space something lurked. But what? The past? Nothingness? Emptiness? I could feel it as much as I could feel say the need to eat when I was hungry, or the sleep I had had the night before. Was it a need then? But I was happy, and life was for living, and this mystery could remain where it was, in its box, inside my mind!

(Were it not that my soul was hungry).

◆ ◆ ◆ ◆ ◆ ◆

I carried my cold beading glass and placed it on a table in the sun and myself on a wooden chair. From where I was sitting I could see in the angle of the white house across the street the window that gave onto the landing of the first floor corridor, but I could not see inside, its glass panes reflecting only the sky outside: an apt metaphor for the opaqueness of my inner mind to myself.

Sipping the beer, looking at the people decorously arrayed about me, I felt oddly displaced, a stranger in an even stranger land – a tourist, a voyeur.

I put on my shades against the glare of the afternoon sun. Well, I had accomplished not one of the tasks I had set myself that day- phone calls, letters, chores: so in a sense this was a holiday; and now draining the last of the lager I gained a fresh euphoria from its bubbles as they burst in concert with the splintered sunlight in my brain.

Or what was left of it. I grinned to myself as I staggered onto the dirt encrusted paving of the street – a girl sitting on the last table on the way out shot me an odd look. I broadened my grin for her benefit. She turned away dismissive of my gesture: common humanity? This was it – the Big City.

And London groaned on its axis – the concreted mass lurched on its horizontal as the sun tipped past its zenith and as I looked back at the café with the girl still seated with her back to me, long shadows stretched their fingers further: the sunny scene was slowly being cast into shade.

I decided then and there to walk back via my flat to pick up any messages and change into a warmer outfit.

Sticking to the sunny side of the street, I wove my way under the lee of the solid Victoriana of the heavy houses of the Westbourne precinct and shot out (as a small barque on a tributary stream shoots out into a main river splintered through with dappled sunlight and slow moving heavy waters) onto Portobello Road.

The flower stall stood in a blaze of sun, the many coloured petals of its multifarious blooms a glory of pulsing light set against the darkening skies up the hill; blues, reds, yellows, lilacs glowing under the row of naked bulbs strung carelessly along the wooden posts of the stall. I let my gaze linger on the sight as I might have on tropical fish amongst the dull of coral. Crowds of people ambled up and down sporting their boho market shab, strange faces from the hood leering out of the backdrop. The coffee shops and tea and chip stalls awash with more folk; market traders were making a din calling out the prices of their wares. I smiled a smile of contentment, one with the scene, and joining the upstream current I was carried up the hill by a stream of jostling people.

Towards the top of Portobello the crowd thinned to a trickle and I turned off and crossed the leafy salubriousness of Ladbroke Square before joining Notting Hill main drag; its squalid architecture and wash of traffic cruising through from the West End to the Oxford road.

I skipped across the flow and through the gauntlet of the two new pizzerias that stood one on either corner of the entrance to my hill – two sirens to the senses, and mounted the steep rise on my side of the street opposite the small row of useful shops that nestled up its beginning, and finally came to the stone steps up to my front door; and the climb up past the other flat's doors, one on each landing, until mine appeared magically before me. The key inserted, the levers tumbled and I was in; my sanctuary, nest, home: back where the story started via semi-circular spirals of navigation – but with still only half the day gone so the rest of the temporal circle to complete – for only in the whole is there sufficiency (unto the day?) – and the world was widely considered flat until it was circumnavigated by the intrepid sailors of yore.

◆　◆　◆　◆　◆　◆

I shed my shoes, emptied my pocket of phone, keys, wallet, onto the hall table, climbed out of my trousers, ripped off my shirt, padded barefoot across the creaky wooden floorplanks and flung myself on the front room sofa, switched on the TV by remote and let the depleted images of the world proffered by CNN wash over my tired mind until I fell into a quick deep slumber.

I climbed aboard the gondola and the gondolier punted down the Grand Canal (and we were surrounded by palaces) not unlike a larger version under more placid skies of the random industrial waterways one can find in the London suburbs. Then he turned up a narrower canal that wound between grassy banks. It turned into a wide square lake: large palaces surrounded it, each of a different colour and design. The water shone an emerald green, with the brilliant turquoises of shallow water above sand beds in the tropics. Opening up off the lake were canals flanked by palaces of such breathtaking grace and beauty that my heart cried out at the perfection. The gondolier rang his bell. I presumed my time was up.

I woke to the phone's ringing.

"Darling! Darling! How is my lovely one! It's me, Justine. I'm at the airport. Do come and pick me up?"

The warmth and vibrancy of her voice added to the translucent brilliance of my dream thrust me into a happy awakening.

"What?" I replied huskily but happily. "Why don't you take the tube in? I didn't know you were coming."

"Why, my Dear – neither did I! How long will you be?" – he could virtually hear her draw deeply on a cigarette. She must have exhaled for she continued: "I'll wait for you at the bar if I'm through before you get here; terminal-."

The phone was dead in his hand as a spent revolver. As usual she left him no option. To be or not to be: with her? His thoughts flew to Viki and her massive potential for jealousy – oh Christ, he thought. Why? Oh, why?

But he knew before he hung up the receiver that he would go.

His body propelled him as though in automaton mode towards shoes, jacket, keys. Then it occurred to him that he had picked up no messages since before meditation class, either on the mobile or the landline.

The heat building now.

Hot white houses on the wide part of Cromwell Road flow past as I drive – and the car rides up like a plane on take-off up onto the elevated flyover; space age upper bodies of buildings loom over the sparse fast moving traffic;

and then we (me and my car) are down again on the A4 , on that familiar 30's carriageway flanked by its mock tudor homes that line every London suburb in a similar flight of early mass townscape fantasy that invariably manages to be slightly depressing; a cheap and mean interpretation of the utopian garden city – a developer's and money man's idea of mass perfection- mile upon mile of it: until it is almost with relief that one rises again above the meanness of ground level out onto the long elevated section that moves out of town through a mix of neo industrial landscape, neo-con office blocks glittering their new money against the skyline and the lost parks of old once country mansions, retreats of the movers and shakers of their classical day, engulfed now by the ever expanding burbs.

As the traffic on the opposing carriageway flashed past, snapshots of Justine flashed across my mind, her face always mobile, animated by her encouraging smile, her body always in the posture of a dancer, her lips always ready with laughter. With this levity she carried the weight of her Latin darkness, her smoldering eyes, raven eye, olive skin – the dark secrets hidden under the omerta of her childhood . . . and so the traffic turns and slows and we dive into the Heathrow tunnel as an (arrow entering the mouth of hell) or: (like Luke Skywalker flying his craft into the black mouth of the mothership).

And out we come into the toytown world of Heathrow and its myriad carparks. And into the terminal and its soft hum if meaningful activity, its cornucopia consumer paradise if miniature shops with everything you ever wanted arranged in plastic reflecting colours off their shelves, to the themed cafés and pubs – so you could sip your coffee your Olde English Ale beneath the beamed ceilings of Shakespeare's London while overhead down through space a craft was landing noiselessly like a ghost ship ready to disgorge its dehumanized cargo into the many concourses and thorofares of this our city's (and the world's) space-age gateway!

◆ ◆ ◆ ◆ ◆ ◆

Waiting, hanging, lurking in front of the arrivals doors, drivers with their placards balanced hopefully in their hands, children milling, coffees being sipped – the scuffed mock marble floor; this brave attempt at the new temple of travel as consumerism didn't quite pull it off: too much drabness and too much anxiety showed through the cracks in its already redundant structure. Glass smeared with dirt, smells, noises, cacophony – an environment in which one maintained oneself in one's bubble – inviolate and pristine, and all the traveling world hurried by (all dressed in their best clean knickers) – and on this level Terminal One worked, as one was automatically thrust into the existential.

This theatre of the absurd continued, as us waiters waited on the side of the barrier designated to us – so many barriers, so many dividing lines all over the place; like a mini simulacrum of society at large. The arrivees drifted through in ones twos and threes, in bunches, then minutes when no one came through the swing doors; doors with one way mirrored glass so we could not see through. When the doors swung open to admit another lost face into this our world we caught glimpses of the nether world of transit purgatory, and each time I made out and in my imagination and tried to fix her form onto one of the distant briefly glimpsed figures before the doors closed again. And in my mind I visualized what she might be wearing, how her smile might light up from a dull worry when she caught sight of me, how I would react, how my posture might be. Odd, these moments of pre-meeting, as though the mind is trying to grapple with a phantom and as the familiar face emerges from its journey towards you from through those interminable swing doors it can for a moment clash with the picture one has been holding, and it is as if one almost has to refocus, reknow the other – and as one walks towards each other, arms outstretched in all probability, her face will hover between smiles until after perhaps a hug and some hurried exchanges of pleasantries and fumbling with cases and direction, the real self of the other emerges in its concreteness, and there she is, to be related to again; reclaimed, reknown, appropriated.

Breaking the reverie I fell to observing the travelers as they came through, walking the gauntlet of us waiters and watchers, with their laden trolleys – a story clinging to each one related by the semaphore of their faces, bodies, clothing, luggage, gestures, language and the aura of happiness or sadness, hope or apprehension that emanated from each one. Some walked on through alone, untouched; wrapped in conversation with a friend or colleague – but the most interesting to observe were the ones who ran onto those meeting them, like two colliding cultures or the sea when it melts into the sands it has been rushing towards for so long.

And I was about to fall into this category of the rushed towards; and maybe someone would be observing me – but whether drawing similar conclusions from their observation; who knows.

Yes. My life was about to become immensely more complicated. And I was looking forward to it – hugely.

CHAPTER SIX: JUSTINE 16:45PM

And here she comes.
It's like she was always there.
Just like in the movies.
Moving from the hip.
And it is not how I imagined...

Her black eyes engulf me so that from across the hall we are straight away each others: there is no gulf of time or space, no time lag – we know each other instantaneously as though we had always been there together, and the busy concourse we are standing in becomes one of those time-less zones, and in its transformation it glows, and becomes a memory even as we clasp, hug, kiss and laugh, there alone on the marbled floor.

Being with the other, in close proximity, being with them as in a permanent (for that moment) presence flickering on my horizon – is as elemental as the day or night, sleep or waking, sun or water. And as with water so with relationships: one enters into it, becomes immersed, sinks or swims; it is hot, it is cold – and the ship of relating, that ark which holds but two souls, afloat on a sinking sea for its forty days and forty nights, until it flounders too onto its Mount Ararat – pinioned by the sheer point of an underwater mountain; an iceberg to the Titanic of love – but with Justine I hesitated to call what we had love. It was more fluid, amorphous, watery than that.

With Viki I had had love: the conventions had been there; the falling in – the rows – the breakups – the getting back together, and the whole had bounced less on each recall, like a slowing bungee jumper, until now we were both left dangling in our harnesses, gently bobbing, twisting in the winds to turn and face each other occasionally, left to wonder if another bounce might reenergize the elastic of the once ecstatic.

Yet I did love Justine.

As we drove out of the gloom of the multi-storey carpark and out into the sunshine, the shadows were already beginning to lengthen into afternoon. The two lane ramp we were driving down curved gently into the sun's rays, its black tarmac split in a curve of light between matt black and a glistening black sparkle that looked almost white in its intensity until one's eyes rose to the stark white glare of the ramp side wall. We were entering the two-tone universe of the sun's first serious descent towards evening, the gay meridian lost in shadows now, the world heaving its weight heedless so that we were falling inadvertently towards the void of night, that great punctuation mark in time's every twenty-four hour passage.

It was with quiet resignation that James observed this, and he saw it as a metaphor for the passing of the mid point of his life, and he wondered gloomily, despite the fact that Justine was now sitting next to him, whether the sun would ever shine at its zenith on his life once more.

And then a moment later as the car followed the curve further full sunlight fell on the windscreen bathing his eyes in blinding light flashing everywhere, and he smiled suddenly, the cloud lifting from his mind.

Justine noticed his smile and laughed, thinking he was smiling at a story she was telling of which he had scarcely been aware.

So depression can cause a rift to open up between people, James thought, and he determined to be cheerful, wondered how such a moment of despondency had seized him in the presence of Justine with all her sparkle, glamour and a supposed blessing to be in. Perhaps it had been caused by a subliminal guilt about Viki? No. Guilt was not there. Worried then. More likely. She was hardly likely to take Justine's arrival in London very happily. Now I will be forced no doubt to choose between the two women I love – and can find no ground for making such a choice. And he felt the choice being thrust upon him – and that he could see no solid reading of the future on which to base his present. The future swam before him. But he pushed these thoughts away as not cheerful so not helpful; but was left with a nagging suspicion that something was wrong as they joined the main concourse of cars onto the M4 into town.

◆ ◆ ◆ ◆ ◆ ◆

…And his determined cheerfulness dispersed the clouds of depression like the sunshine a brief summer storm, and it lifted just as Justine was beginning to furrow her brow at James's long pauses and lack of repartee; it was as though he had taken a sudden gulp of oxygen – the smile he had been forcing onto his face set, and radiated his inner being. He relaxed and heaved a sigh of relief that his black mood had been so brief and of little immediate consequence.

"Are you all right?" Justine spoke hesitantly.

"Yes. Oh yes!" he could answer honestly.

Justine sat back in her seat seemingly content with his explanation.

◆ ◆ ◆ ◆ ◆ ◆

The traffic was flowing easily over the elevated road that curved through the outer parts of west London – Osterley, Ealing, passing anonymously below us, their facelessness only punctuated by the glossy glass towers of corporate egoism that flashed past at regular intervals. The elevated section began its swoop down towards Chiswick.

"And is she still in your life?"

I paused. Was Justine implying that something might lie between me and her? – it never had yet on the physical plane; or was she merely being cheeky, joshing me about Viki and our supposedly 'bad' relationship which in many ways it was – what little relating that still remained to it.

"The thing is," I replied, taking the above reflection into account: "why are you interested?"

"Oh James, how can you ask that?" she said self-consciously slyly, leaning over and pecking me on the cheek.

What did this mean. Yes or no? That she wanted to take us further, or that I was being ridiculous. Presumptuous.

Possibly… I was no nearer clarity. I felt like talking to her about Viki. But it would be a mistake. Honesty, so tempting a concept, in reality became so often a big mouth. She would not respond rationally to my philosophical enquiries about my affair with another woman

Or would she? That was the question. ~ Only one way to find out. Flush her out. Was she for me or against me or didn't she care. Or perhaps she would dissemble and I would be fooled. Or I wouldn't be. The geometry of the whole thing was way beyond me. The rational cut no ice here. Relax and enjoy the ride then, a little voice said:

This time I'd get the donkey's head in front of its tail.

And this time I was not going to get it wrong!

Such inner determination always worried me. Can will-power alter the course of fate, or does its exercise only drag one further in the wrong direction? My mind felt tired, so instead of further thought I let my hand slide into hers and felt the warmth of contact, the electricity flow quietly between us...

and I slow down letting the fast traffic push aggressively past and in the shallows on the edge of the road I drift the car, sun blinding in the rear mirror, long shadows casting across our path like trees on a riverbank on some long forgotten summer day: falling so deep into reverie that I think of stopping the car so unsure am I of my touch with reality all of a sudden... and flashes of Viki and her thin smile, wide but thin, and the madness that hovers over her features like a veil, a cover for the inner her that I try and believe is good, sane. And I feel torn – torn between these two women both of whom I belong with and yet in different ways are not mine: Viki through the self centeredness of her damaged brain and Justine through our (as yet) lack of physical proximity.

I suggested that we pull off the carriageway and take one of the side turnings and visit the river. Justine nodded assent. Her face wore a contented smile, as though she was happy in that moment, absorbed by what she was seeing/feeling.

It felt as though a curtain had fallen between events and my mind: I was being carried by events as by a river – my thoughts completely separate from what was going on – a commentary only.

Flashing on the meditation class: I feel myself being drawn inexorably towards that inner space I found for a moment there but had ignored at the time. In a way it felt the most real moment of the day so far, as though all the rest was a dream whirl of external events; leaves on the wind tossed idly to float away on the streams of time. The inner space felt like a quiet hall where I resided, armchair by the fireside at home: and I wanted to be in that place more, again, and rest from my mind there…

Someone blared a horn at me; "Watch the road", Justine gasped grabbing me by the wrist – but oddly my reverie stayed with me, enduring this sudden barrage from the outside world; and I smiled, feeling oddly comforted.

I pulled the car up and parked smoothly. We walked an alley together, me and Justine, between the sides of tall old houses. Ahead a tall rectangle of light opened out like a fan as we approached to reveal a greying sky and a smudge of water flowing in a trough beneath it: it was low tide.

Wind blew my hair as we entered through the swing doors of a riverside pub. Outside the trees tossed in the sudden new wind. Inside we watched the weather nursing beers sat by a large window in the empty establishment, only the barman polishing glasses quietly at the gloomy bar at the back of the room.

"What a cold afternoon; how the weather has changed," said James shivering as the clouds blew across a grey sky outside.

"Oh James, how English you are: talking about the weather."

"I felt cold," he replied limply. But he smiled; what she said was most probably true. What was it with the English, about this country – its greying skies entered one's very bones. They finished their beers and strolled outside. Even the river, father Thames was grey and low. It shouldn't be like this, James thought. He looked up and high in the sky to the west, above the main Heathrow flightpath with its drone-like line of jetliners following each other on their descent paths, a large patch of blue was opening up in the heavens. And as he watched the high winds blew the ragged clouds apart and the blue patch became massive so that the westering sun was revealed and shone through warming his face.

"So changeable your English weather." She had taken his hand without him noticing. Now he felt its warmth flow through him.

"Like her men?"

"Yes; they are so moody under that stiff upper lip."

"Really."

"Yes really" – and she took him in her arms and folded him into an embrace to which he felt himself responding, breathing deeper – and then her mouth was on his.

They walked hand in hand alone on the river promenade with its uneven paving, patches of tarmac and shallow steps. The houses behind the promenade were ivy clad, English gardened, French windows opening onto Edwardian balconies on first floors, all charm, proportion and prosperous domesticity.

They strolled and turned back for the car. James felt a panic arising from his stomach area. Christ. What to do? Viki would fly at him; it would be over, that door closed. And this door, opened a crack now by this Latin woman so different from the northern warrior Viki – where might that lead? He breathed deeply and let his mind back to the inner space of meditation. But it was no good – his mind raced out of that room so unused was it to sitting there, and his mental anguish redoubled. They turned into the alley leading away from the river and back to his car. He relaxed into different part of his mind that only thought how pleasant it was to be held by the hand by this gorgeous, vibrant woman. Her kiss lingered in him both a charge and a connection. Be damned to complications; he thought bravely to himself.

He felt soft with passion as they stopped in the alley and fell into each other's arms once more. The drive back to his flat was like a moment wrapped in time. Both their bodies knew that they were only waiting for something to happen; The Thing. Yet it seemed so unreal that it would as they rushed towards that seminal moment, running lights that turned to red as they fled through the unbusy junctions of West London

"Careful James."

"Yes; Miss Moneypenny."

The car screamed to a halt.

They were at each other's clothes on the stairs. He dropped her bag a number of times. It was a slow, luxurious ascent.

The cat meeowed a polite hello seemingly oblivious to the adult ritual taking place before it. Their clothes off, naked, they found the bed and tumbling on it fell into a full embrace and textures and sounds and inner feelings. Limbs curled and flesh came alive. There was no going back now. Her body was more beautiful to the touch than it had looked clothed at the airport: it was an aesthetic paradise, and it was his, he was immersed in it, so here and now that the words had no more meaning. So they played. And walking around the flat, eating forbidden fruits from the fridge, feeding each other, lying and caressing again, watching each other's bodies from a distance, measuring the form with the eye against the touch; and the cat brushing its tail nonchalantly against their ankles as it walked past hoping that all this commotion would lead to its bowl being refilled (in this hope it was fulfilled as both human creatures, sated by their mutual passion felt a beneficence to all God's creatures – the cat was fed twice in the space of ten minutes).

With the promise of more love-making to come later, the exploration of possibilities only begun, James pulled some clothes on. Out on the street there was a soft electric charge as though it was three in the morning and it had just rained; though it was quarter to six and the sun was dipping in a cloudy but blue sky. The car flowed smoothly down to Chelsea as he made his way to his rendezvous with Viki.

James

CHAPTER SEVEN: VIKI 5:59PM

It may seem peculiar that a man should visit a woman he is involved with after making passionate love to another. But to a student of human nature it comes as no surprise. A man no sooner gains one thing than his lust for others is vastly expanded, and once the impulse to monogamy is broken it is not easily mended.

So we find with James as he parks his car up in the salubrious streets of Chelsea, though he himself is probably not aware of the above. So far was James from any such kind of reflection as he slammed his car door shut and with a springy yet languid step advanced down the side of the square towards number ten, that he would have been surprised if you had mentioned it to him.

He felt good. That was the main thing. He had never felt better. What he was going to say or do with Viki he had not the foggiest; only that she should be seen, as he had arranged to see her and wanted so to do. His mind was light and empty in a pleasant frame as he leant on her bell, and the familiar buzz admitted him through the front door.

The squalid lift rattled him up to the top floor where he stepped out of its opening doors into a world of light and luxury that was Viki's den. She had stripped the whole top floor of walls and in place of its roof installed glass reaching high above, plants climbing up towards the light, galleries and sun decks drawing the eye up, the room hot from the afternoon sun despite the open doors, windows and louvres with their sail like blinds drawn here and there against the glare. She was on the polished light wood floor, watering can in hand, a cloth wrapped round her waist and bare breasted, a costume (minus watering can) that she liked to adopt in summer at home!

"Oh it's you!" she said with just enough enthusiasm to tempt me away from the lift and into the room. Had she sensed something through the ether? James was also conscious of her beauty then; her long flaxen hair falling to her slim waist, her long shapely legs and proud profile – so different from the rounded Latin warmth of Justine.

To his surprise James felt a surge of desire for her such as he had not felt for months. She was going about watering the flowers paying scant attention to him. He took his shoes off.

"Take your shoes off dear," she called out in her aristocratic tones.

"I already have!"

She turned and graced him with her beatific smile, what he loved about her – it always lingered after it was gone as though an inner radiance remained in her. Her thin lips swept right up into the curve of a crescent moon, and her large almond coloured eyes looked out sweetly from either side of an aquiline nose.

He went to her and put his hands around her thin waist and nuzzled her warm neck.

"What's got into you?" she craned her face round to catch his eye, smiling mischievously.

"Dunno." And he didn't.

But smiling she came towards him until her beatific smile swam out of focus and her eyes crossed up and down like an early Picasso portrait of one of his mistresses. Then they were a tangle of limbs on the sofa – a tender and manic moment uniting them briefly in love one more time.

Lying on the sofa staring up at the clouds scudding overhead the sun lighting up their western sides great puffball of blinding white, James realized he wanted to be out on the street and get on with his day; above all he needed to think and he felt constrained by Viki's post coital embrace of him; her warm breath shallow and contented, her smile loving, her eyes dreamy. He felt it churlish just to leave; to toss her aside, so he suggested they go for a stroll in the balm of the summer evening air.

Together in the lift as it lumbered downwards to earth. James stared in the mirror. All intimacy seemed to have vanished. He stared at the pair of them in the mirror; they could have been two strangers, or lovers to be about to address their first remarks to each other in the emptiness of a lift. His reverie was broken however when her hand took his in an intimacy that showed them already bound.

Out into the flood of sunlight. The paving stones were strangely warm for so mild a day: there was heat in the sun when it shone. They walked together up the shaded street with its young trees dwarfed by the sheer sides of the large houses.

Out on the Fulham Road they headed down the Beach at a leisurely pace, past the cinema, the coffee shop, the bookshop. James breathed easier. It felt natural to be walking with his longtime partner; nuances of alienation frayed and crumbled. He looked at her face and recognized so much. A wife is always a stranger. A wife is for life. Why was she so keen on marriage? To bind, to entrap, to spoil? With her it lacked romantic sentiment – all was reduced to the realism of survival; the Darwinian par excellence.

"Hey James, Viki, what a wonderful surprise!" James raised his head and there in front of them blocking the pavement was Theo Lansdowne in one of his outstretched arms an ebony cane with a silver top. He wore a black hat and coat and a black scarf was wrapped beneath his white goatee of a beard. The crinkles round his eyes glistened. There was no way past him. Timidly smiling behind him stood the languorous Hermione dressed lightly and elegantly for summer unlike the bulky sweating figure of Theo. She stood so thin, wandish and poised. From between them pushed Madeleine. They all were so slightly drunk.

Theo seemed to have exhausted his capacity for speech with his lustrous hello; as his arms sank to his sides again Madeleine, never a shrinking violet, took over:

"Are you coming to the opening; Andrew Pilkington's you know. Montagu will be there! We're walking there now. Come with us?"

Her warmth was contagious. It was as though despite the vacuousness of her remarks one longed to remain in her company as one did a fire in winter. I glanced at Viki. Her eyes swivelled as though she were watching her own movie screen close up, conveying nothing.

We fell in with them, backtracking the way we had come. Theo fell in next to Viki as he expressed the greatest admiration for her. When it was not drowned out by the roaring of a passing bus, the street echoed to his 'oh my dears' and 'darlings' and 'that's too too gorgeouses' and 'you are so talented and beautiful'. She lapped it up and liked him for it. It was so so nice being paid so much attention.

I walked between Hermione and Madeleine. Madeleine was in a quiet, contemplative mood all of a sudden – so I got the chance to converse with Hermione as we went. We crossed the Fulham Road and walked a quiet side street that wound down towards the Kings road. I always enjoyed Hermione. Her impeccable politeness and consideration was peppered with a wit of surprising lewdness: her remarks were sharp and her satire remorseless. I thought perhaps it had something to do with the past hurt and disappointment that was engraved in the premature lines on her pretty face and the stoop to her well-knit body and which nevertheless she carried so well. There was something so honest about life's emotional scars worn so openly. I knew a little of her past: a father lost in the call of duty, a mother remarried and a family lost; or some such thing: with a creature as delicate and vulnerable as Hermione it seemed crass to pry.

"So what happened after I left?" I asked.

"Where did you go off to then?"

"To the airport to pick up a friend." I stopped. There was so much more behind this remark than it outwardly expressed. Viki too was only a few paces ahead and Madeleine's well trained ear was sure to pick something up. Sure enough, on cue: "Who did you pick up?"

"Oh, just a friend," I deflected.

"After you left?" Madeleine was luckily more interested in her domestic dramas than in any hint her fine social nose had scented about my airport run. "Jim came round, you know, that ex boyfriend of Montagu's. I am afraid that Biggus Dickus story came out again," Madeleine did not look in the least afraid: she was enjoying the scandal. She cast an eye at Hermione.

"Don't look at me," Hermione protested.

"Well someone brought it up. Jim became agitated, accused Monty of ignoring him in those plaintive little Australian tones of his. It's true. Monty is not interested in him; barely likes him. So Jim picks a row with Jerry Rafael. Oh my dear, Jerry was so drunk with his guitar he scarcely noticed Jim's obnoxious behaviour towards him. This enraged Jim further." Hermione was sniggering behind her hand.

"So he pulled down his trousers there in the room in front of all of us. I didn't look," said Hermione taking up the yarn. "See," he yelled. "It's not so big! He was really furious. Everyone laughed. Jim stormed out in a temper. We were all in a fine humour after that. I say, I didn't start the whole thing?" asked Hermione, suddenly embarrassed.

"No my dear. I am sure it was Monty. Well at least he and Dulcie are friends again. She does so lose it so often, poor dear."

"Her own worst enemy," I remarked.

CHAPTER EIGHT:
THE GALLERY 6:13PM

We continued down the next street. Theo and Viki were way ahead now. He was waving his arms about, his cane wagging dangerously. She had her profile turned towards him attentively; then she tossed her head, long hair flying like a horse's tail and resettling a mane of gold hiding her face from us. Near the bottom of the street it emptied out into the Kings Road. Before this confluence was a small art gallery, two old shops joined together so their windows mismatched, one long and low with many small panes of glass set into its old wooden frame, the other a large sheet glass window. Inside people holding glasses were pressed together. The noise of their chatter could be heard from where they were some hundred yards north. Light spilled out into the now shadowed street echoing the blue strip of sky above as though a shaft of the westering sun had been caught inside the gallery and leapt out into the street.

Ahead they saw Theo and Viki stop in the melee outside the gallery door; the party had spilled into the street: people were smoking and drinking there, sat on the wall, standing on the pavement, leant on parked cars. As they drew near them (approaching the distant small town from across the shingle, it comes into clarity slowly, part separating part from part like the pixels of a computer generated image, separating into greater and more detail, as trudging slow I push closer to its embrace) James had one of those flashes he had been there before: but he was on a windswept beach in Suffolk, gulls crying in his ears. He tried to exclude a droning remark from Madeleine from his hearing so he could hold the image, walking with his eyes half closed so the figures in the pool of light outside the gallery window seemed to dance in an out of focus, a haze as they grew larger and nearer. Then he had Theo's heavy arm draped over his shoulder as he was being introduced to a lady. He tried to bring her face into focus. He noticed Viki had moved inside and was already engaged in an animated conversation with a short man in mouse coloured jacket and tie, his small black eyes in a strangely misshapen head, hair thin and obviously home cut. He sighed inwardly. The lady was talking to him. Theo had moved off noisily to his next prey on the pavement. Coming into focus he saw a young and pretty face; very old fashioned whether by artifice or nature he could not immediately tell: she was heavily powdered anyhow, and her clothes had the air of the nineteen-thirties, an Evelyn Waughesque whiff. James smiled involuntarily. She took up his smile and amplified it warmly. When she spoke her voice was richly modulated (in one so young: he thought).

"…I do make shoes," he caught the tail end of what she was saying, finally coming up to speed with his presence there at the gallery. He pushed away the last sounds of the ocean that still echoed disturbingly from his thought flash of moments before.

"Shoes? Yes. I am very pleased with my Chelsea boots!"

To his surprise she squatted down and felt his feet as he stood there in his soft suede hunters, with a blind man's touch: "They are well made, extremely, and they must be so comfortable. If a man in not to wear brogues then Chelsea will do." The woman was astonishing: even her words had a haunting oddity as though cast from another era into a contemporary idiom. As she raised herself her tight fawn trousers displayed the most succulent and promising shapes, round and straight harmonized in the right proportions. He pushed such thoughts rapidly from his mind: seventeen, eighteen, twenty, he couldn't tell. And if to confirm his doubt a burly chap sauntered up the look of worried ownership of a beautiful and delicate object in his eye. He was introduced as the boyfriend. He wondered for a moment as she coyly smiled herself out of his presence to follow the boyfriend what she was doing with such a sweaty lout. No accounting for taste. Probably she was betraying her youth by her choice of him: she would grow out of him. His mind was ripped from these conjectures and his gaze from her sweet posterior by the loud and unmistakable arrival of the massive black becloaked and hatted figure of Montagu Withnail Smith. He bowed and cursed and hullaballooed all in the same breath, stamping his massive booted feet and grabbing a full glass of wine off an acquaintance before passing it back empty. In his train was dancing alongside and around him like a sprite to king Oberon the slight figure of a wrinkled woman with a shaven head all dressed in black tight shirt and trousers which showed a body lithe and strong; her eyes sparkled with warmth and mischief and most of her utterances were at least semi devotional. This was Monty's mother, the famed 'KarMa' Carmen who had wooed and wowed the diplomatic circuit in her younger days.

Through the window his eye was caught by the shock of straw coloured hair that was Viki. She was talking to a woman now. The woman moved into his line of vision and to his shock it was Justine. Horror shock. His mouth went dry and he mostly ignored the chirping smile of KarMa saying hello to him. But then he felt himself fast relaxing. So what if they did compare notes? It might prove educational. It need not be bad. KarMa was still making chirping noises and James now bantered with her, only a corner of one eye drifting through the window now and again.

KarMa, or plain Ma as she liked to be addressed, was a lively intelligence who had the refreshing qualities of cutting through nonsense like a knife, and also of being invariably positive; even being stuck in a rainstorm in a car in a traffic jam would be fun if she was there to enlighten it.

A slight chill blew up the street. Overhead the leaves danced on a massive old tree. A lamp-post had already come on over the shaded side of the street. The day had not quite died into night.

"See what I got!" said Ma in her forever foreign accent, grinning her mischievous grin. From out of a pocket hidden in the folds of her shirt she withdrew like a magician a little box. She pulled its lid off and took out a joint which she lit with a flourish and then blew out a large cloud of pungent smoke. She passed it to James who took a few token puffs not wishing to appear churlish. "Have you been to the zen gardens?" she went on; "in Holland Park, so beautiful. You walk round and over a little bridge under which the water

flows from the waterfall. There you leave the past behind!"
She snapped her fingers and grinned.

"How nice. I'd like to do that," said James wistfully.

"You can!"

"I can't see myself going to Holland park in the near future."

"Forget the future! Live in the now! Leave the past: no need to go to zen garden for that!"

She ballooned another great halo of smoke that billowed around her so that for a moment James had a vision of a small deity floating in the clouds a magical grin spread across her face.

He pushed on through the crowd at the door and squeezed through people until he was inside. Suddenly he needed a drink; whether it was to douse the slight narcotic effect of his slight inhalation or because of his fright at the two women (there they were close, in a dense growth of figures in the window corner of the forest of figures) or simply because it was sundowner time or a mixture of all three, he had not space to conjecture as all his concentration was taken by the fight towards the bar. There was white wine, red wine, orange juice and what looked like water. He grabbed a white; it was warm and half full: more reliable than cheap red though, which would taste like old stewed prunes. It tasted lemony and refreshing enough. He took a gulp and felt better. He peered through the swaying and moving forest and caught flashing impressions of parts of both of them: a streak of Viki's fair hair, a splash of her white dress with its red and blue patterning, one eye suddenly revealed: no chance it would focus on him – he was as though hidden peering through the trunks. Justine's dark hair was more visible but more indistinct. He hovered near the bar, finished his glass and took another.

His elbow was gently shaken. He turned and saw Jerry Rafael standing there in his shabby suit looking every inch the bohemian retired major. His face was melting in the stupor of his soaked state; his eyes swam, he wore a brand new pare of bright red rock'n roll pumps of which he was inordinately proud. He thrust them forward and stared at them inviting me to follow his gaze. "Let go of my arm, my wine is spilling," I said abruptly.

"Oh sorry, here, let me get you another, nice shoes, is that your bird over there, must speak to Luke… " his thought disordered ramble continued but was drowned out by the cacophony of voices calling all around.

"Can't hear!"

"Oh sorry, but I must get you that glass… "

"No, it's all right, it's still quite full."

"Can you get me one, the crowd, can't push." And indeed he was swaying and wobbling most unsteadily in his shoes. I placed my glass in his hand and pushed through and retrieved a full one. When I got back to him his lips were glistening, my glass was dangling from his fingers empty.

"Give me my glass."

"But it's empty."

"I can see that. Pass it to me please."

"Oh sorry, oh yes." He stared at his hand holding the empty glass a moment then his brain connected with his hand and the glass was passed to me. I poured half the wine from the new glass into the old glass and handed him back the old glass. He took it looking at me sideways: "Very sneaky," he said. I was about to reply a little angrily but his attention had wandered again: "my guitar, left it at the Troubadour, can you go and get it for me?"

"Why's it there?" I asked not wishing to get dragged in or off.

"Money owing. Thought I had this wad of cash on me."
He searched his pockets then shrugged. "Very rude to me.
Manager said I owed hundreds of quid. Said I had bought
everybody drinks."

"Had you?"

"Can't remember." He looked at me hopelessly.

"So, to get your guitar I'd have to pay hundreds?"

"Talk to him. I'll have the money soon. Owing to me.
My solicitor. Must have guitar. Need to play. Oh my God,
if there really is one…" he began to hum, then trailed off.
"Goes something like that…" Food stains covered his shirt
and his hat was crushed beyond battered. It was a wonder that
he was still alive.

The crowd surged and then separated us. I was half carried
and set down relatively nearer Viki and Justine. I could see
more of both of them, most in fact, and if one of them were to
take the time off from haranguing the other they would have
seen me there; for their conversation looked quite heated now
compared with the placid scene I had witnessed through the
window. I wondered whether now was the moment to intervene. Here and now, I heard the echo of KarMa's voice, 'here
and now'; like the parrot in Aldous Huxley's 'Island', constantly calling one to attention. Well here and now I did not
feel like getting any closer to the two of them. I was saved
by Theo.

"My dear boy," he announced. protruding his belly in my
direction. He looked quite distinguished with his wavy white
hair and neatly clipped beard; only his face was blotched with
too much drink and good living. "Always such a pleasure to
see you, such an honour to be able to talk to you. You are one
of the special people, you know. Part of the club." He almost
winked. While it was always nicer to be complimented than
ignored or insulted I found his remarks jarred rather. What

was I meant to respond? So I didn't. "Fine show!" he spoke into my silence. I looked at the canvases in their frames behind glass on the walls where I could see them in the spaces between the verticals of people. They appeared standard Chelsea gallery fare much as a newspaper might reveal standard newspaper fare. On closer examination no doubt I might find an investment of appreciation would pay me back by heightening their artistic worth to me. Their monetary worth £600 there £500 there as I could see from their stickers would be less susceptible to further meditation.

"It is quite good," I mumbled.

"Yes!" boomed Theo, throwing in a chuckle for effect. But I could tell he was being totally insincere.

"I meant the crowd, the party. Haven't looked at the pictures yet!"

Theo laughed to give himself time to think of the appropriate reply. "You are a rascal!" he finally said in an avuncular fashion and draped his arm over my shoulder to show the world we were friends. I could see I might have quite as much trouble with him as with Jerry. I wanted a period to contemplate my two women (hardly a subject I could share with Theo's loud mouth).

"Look at that one," I pointed at a nondescript splodge of reddy browns. I moved over to the wall and resolutely stared at it. Theo looked nonplussed by this behaviour and with a "Catch you later my boy!" lumbered off. Since there was nothing else to do and I wished to stay closeish to the two ladies, I fell to looking at the canvass in front of my nose, price £700. It was a sort of post Rothkoish pastiche, mixed with something of the individual style the painter, who was apparently a woman from her name on the card below the price and title of the work, must have developed over the long years of artistic struggle of her career. The result was a mixture of the mystical and naive with a technical proficiency that might have been self developed or adopted, I knew not. The whole was dreary and confusing, though decorative enough and well executed enough to hang in a contemporary room as a minor decoration. A lady was now standing next to me sharing my contemplation. She glanced at me shyly. She was slight and plump and wore glasses. She hesitantly asked me whether I liked it. I answered noncommittally. We chatted fairly amiably for a few moments. Her name rang a bell; I glanced at the card. She was the artist. "Why did you call this one 'Nebuchadnezzar's Feast' I asked politely.

"Can't you see!" the small, plump woman answered me testily.

I peered at the picture again hoping for instant illumination. There were what might have been cross motifs in one corner. Had Nebuchadnezzar something to do with crosses? Hadn't he been a king of Babylon? What had he done? Was it Daniel and the fire? There was no representation of fire on the canvass, nor of kings, enslaved Israelites, lions, nor Babylon. James looked at the artist with a defeated expression. But the difficult extrication from the rapidly deepening impasse that they both faced accomplishing in a socially acceptable manner was voided by the sound of two raised female voices. James wished he could carry on talking with the artist for however tricky the ground they trod it was nothing to what he would have to face now. But the artist's attention had turned from her still canvas to the real life passion being played out before them.

A small space had cleared around Viki and Justine. Viki was soaked with wine so her nipples showed through her now transparent, clinging white top. James felt sorry for her dripping there, shaking wine droplets from her hands, that is until she opened her mouth: "You bitch," she shrieked in a

truly hideous voice. She took hold of Justine's collar. Justine
was just standing there the offending well aimed empty glass
in her hand, no doubt astounded at the effectiveness of the
wine in humiliating her opponent. But now it was Viki's turn.
She was both large and strong: she ripped Justine's collar
and stood back an ugly glare on her face. The crowd gasped.
People were pressed up against the window outside. James
saw Monty's face, and Ma's. Justine's top fell open expos-
ing a round breast. She had to use the hand which was not
holding the glass to hold up the material over the offending
part. But she was not finished. Probably Viki's non-stop glare
re-provoked her. Justine deftly, almost in one quick movement so as to strike once more before the battle was declared
over, dropped her garment again so her breast burst forth and
swiping a glass from an astounded gentlemen flung its liquid
contents at Viki's face. But Viki was ready. She ducked aside
and only a small splash of wine caught the side of her hair
and face. The rest sailed on through the air in an elongated
body and splattered in an uncompromising splash all over
Nebuchadnezzar's Feast.

"At least it's red wine!" called out some wag. Everyone
laughed. Perhaps the picture would be improved. The artist
looked distressed and disappeared. The crowd lost interest
and its normal hubbub began again at an even higher pitch.
They all had a good story to take on with them now. The gallery owner should pay Viki and Justine, I thought.

But she had marched over, and in her fierce tweeds she
looked none too amused. Bohemian behaviour most be kept
strictly to the canvasses. The picture was wrecked. James felt
that it was all his fault. He supposed now was the time to
intervene. Better late than never. Against the window faces
were pressed like flowers, high and low, big and small, waving and bobbing as though tossed in a wind. Amongst them

he saw Madeleine, Hermione, Ma and Jerry, all with identical expressions as though they were watching the same scene in a film and were responding identically to the director's cue. The crowd of faces seemingly bodiless in the dimness of the street was counterpointed by the empty brightness of the interior they were voyeuring; that end of the gallery had mostly cleared. The end by the door was still crowded but was fast emptying. Shards of broken glass lay glistening on the white floor like shells on a beach deserted after a sudden storm. Withnail Smith was mouthing something at him from through window and gesturing imperiously, but James could not follow him; he felt suddenly tired. He wondered if it would be inappropriate to grab another glass of wine off the bar. He walked over and taking a glass wandered over to the fractious pair, two spent gladiators panting alone in the empty arena. Viki was still wet, standing in her drips looking around (for a cloth?) and her nipples still stood out in all their beauty under their damp, transparent veil. Justine was still holding up her dress with one hand, wandering around as though in a daze, muttering. Two or three ineffectual gentleman hovered at a safe distance looking concerned.

"Well, that buggered up the evening!" James said, finally making the twosome a threesome.

"Fucked, not buggered," muttered Justine still not looking at either of them. Had she lost something on the floor?

"Very droll, fat Latino," Said Viki petulantly.

"Would you mind!" a fierce voice barked forcefully and angrily. "I won't have such language in here! Who are you people?"

"Em… " answered James. He was staring straight into the eyes of the gallery owner, a formidable transatlantic woman in her fifties. She was not amused at all. She sneered at James's fresh glass of 'her' wine. Behind her was the plump artist, visibly distressed, her spectacles steamed up.

"Oh, Jemima! Let me introduce my friends! This is James Low, and here being wet is Viki; how are we Viki?" Viki nodded at Montagu who had glided up. Behind him came his mother, smiling and relaxed.

"If these are friends of yours!" barked the tweeded Jemima, not mollified at all, "you should take them out of here!"

"I shall, I shall," said Montagu beaming; "Would you all care to dine with me? I have a table reserved, by chance, at the Arts Club." Jemima glared at Monty. He was rewarding the miscreants and she had wanted to throw them out into the street disgraced. "Would you care to join us, Jemma?"

Jemima struggled for a moment: an invitation to the Chelsea Arts was not to be lightly thrown down.

"No, I can't," she said quietly; and to the others: "You've wrecked my evening. It's only eight and everyone has fled. It's a disaster. I want you to pay for that picture!" She walked over to her desk which was by the door.

Montagu struck a pose and nibbled a finger nail while surveying the scene. "Better get these girls wrapped up," he finally said.

Viki and Justine unfroze, the tableau broken and time running its normal course once more. Withnail and I went over to survey the damaged Nebuchadnezzar. "Now actually worth £700 after the alterations made by your Justine," he commented sotto voce. The other end of the room the girls were being helped by a grudging Jemima into spare tops aided by Ma. Suddenly voices were raised again; Jemima's loud drawl and Justine's staccato base Latin. Monty raised his eyebrows and looked at me. I restrained welling laughter. He suppressed a smile: "Come, we are called on again."

Justine was refusing to pay Jemima seven hundred pounds. Ma wasn't helping by saying: "But they made your party a go go; it was so dull before… " Jemima was becoming more frosty by the moment.

Jerry wobbled in through the open door to add his bit. "Seems a bit steep, seven-hundred, how about sevenny – it is damaged ya know, the paint..." he slurred before his drunken legs carried him back out into the street again (where at least he belonged).

"Give me the bill then," Justine finally said giving way, stretching out her hand. Jemma sat down behind her desk and took up her pen and began writing out a slip. Viki looked quizzically at Justine. But Justine gave nothing away. We all crowded round behind her. The invoice was handed over. "And my picture?" said Justine coolly. But she had pushed too far with this shot. "You can have it when your cheque clears," snapped Jemma. Everyone was aware there would be no cheque and this whole farce was a face saving charade.

"See you again, darling!" Ma called into the gallery as we tumbled out. I heard no answer.

James

CHAPTER NINE: THE CLUB 8:04 PM

We all stopped in the street. Justine and Viki were smiling at each other. Suddenly we were all in hysterics. The gallery door was slammed shut.

"Oh, poor Jemima," said Withnail stifling a last chuckle behind his hand. The two girls flung their arms around each other and hugged. As we sauntered down to the corner of the Kings Road which seemed the logical direction in which to go, towards the traffic and lights, cafés and shops, bustle and noise, they remained in each others arms laughing, chatting, giggling. "Charming," Monty commented.

"What about the Arts Club?" I asked.

"Oh, that! No reservation; not even a member... "

We caught up with Madeleine and Hermione on the

corner. Jerry we had left behind in the gutter: he was too drunk to follow.

"What happened in there?" asked Madeleine. We all related the story together. She looked from one to the other of us. Hermione wasn't quite sure whether to be amused or censorious. Finally Madeleine nodded her head; "fine way to carry on! Jemma is a close friend of mine, I'll have to call her in the morning. Where are we off to now?" with which she effectively snapped the subject closed.

"Witnail Smit is takin us to the Farts Club," said Justine all helpful smiles. Madeleine sighed. "The Art's Club. He's not a member dear. But I am. I am sure Boris can find us a table. Come on dears," she called and trotted forward a little girl again. All was forgiven. All was forgotten. Madeleine was in her element.

The quiet tree lined street, the long low house, the little door and cosy lobby, and through to a scene cut straight out of Edwardian England, only missing the waistcoats and walrus moustaches popular of that period. A large high room, galleried on one side, a small bar nestling into its end invitingly, French windows opening onto leafy gardens and a vast billiard table upon which two gentlemen were working their cues. Madeleine led us to a table under the French windows where we lounged with our drinks. A dining table had been found for us, whether by the offices of one Boris or not, out in the garden. I had often suspected Madeleine of affecting a familiarity with the likes of barmen and shopkeepers which was not wholly founded in reality; she had no doubt adopted it from some character from a book or a movie.

Out in the garden fairy lights danced in the trees. Around the tables a soft murmur of voices arose as from beneath a sea. I wandered away into the gloom beneath the grand trees and bathed myself in the peace and softness there. Overhead the first evening stars shone in a sky deepening to purple. A plane cruised across the sky to the south, its lights winking; hundreds of people in there, I thought; what aboriginal staring up would have guessed it, taken it for anything but a heavenly body. Strange thing time: there we were witnessing that fracas in the gallery and it was all so real and only moments ago; yet it has vanished from this earth never to be repeated as much as any other moment consigned to history. Perhaps that is what makes each moment golden, especially after it is over – its uniqueness; even the worst moment holds some promise for a future looking back on it with some glimmer of fondness. He kicked at the grass and then squatted, listening to the night noises. It occurred to him he still did not know what Justine and Viki knew of him vis a vis each other.

They were the best of friends now, sitting next to each other, the blonde and the brunette, laughing at the same jokes, turning their heads in unison, ordering the same food and drink, beginning their sentences at the same time then both stopping with a giggle to give way to the other. James had never seen so fast a transformation.

He sat on a low garden chair. The faces of his friends were bathed in candle light, or was it the deep last shaft of the setting sun refracting down from the sky so blue it was virtually black. Hunched round the table, talking softly, they appeared to James as a picture: a Stanley Spencer of the idealized English pastoral life; a medieval portrait of happy prosperity, simple but kind. He knew he was fantasizing; but that remove only made his reverie that much more contenting: the dulcet tones of Madeleine's voice was wafting him into a happy somic state; he felt his brain soften into a state of semi opiate buzz – only the picture of the faces and the candle and the darkness gathering round, the soothing sound of soft voices – remained in his mind: all else was a happy void.

He sat on in this state for some minutes, watching a waiter bring a bottle of wine and open it and place it in a cooler. "What will you have?" Madeleine called over to him. "Oh, you order for me," he replied, his reverie unbroken by being drawn into the scene.

After some minutes he climbed out of the garden chair and wandered across the dim grass towards the French windows and the warm glow of light inside the club. He wandered through the bar room. The same two gentlemen were still playing billiards. The room was empty apart from a fat man sat at the bar and the barman quietly talking with him. It was as though time had stopped while they had been outside. He saw a sign saying toilets. He pushed through a swing door. There was a small lobby with a deep armchair. A pile of newspapers lay beside it. A clock was ticking on the wall. A dim light flickered overhead. He slumped into the old armchair. He let his mind range. He imagined all the paths he might have trod in life if he had taken different turns at certain moments – all those parallel lives unlived

As another summer
falls on this land of nod
and I
sitting here
inside, in the old armchair
think of times past,
remembered now without attachment...
those dead lanes
reserved only to memory,
which my feet never trod

And yet
if there is a truth,
is it that I can feel it

sitting here in high summer
alone
stranded on a high rise beach
in this city of insanity?

That you are still with me
whispering yourself
barely felt
a perceptible tingle
like a present memory
So close now
in this
The long night of my soul

all those parallel lives unlived… yet perhaps to be lived again.

The pleasant sensation of the garden had worn off so completely it was as though it had never been. The opium had worn off and the dream had vanished to be replaced?… to be replaced by a morbid imagining. He struggled with it a moment, sitting bolt upright in the chair as though a dentist were approaching him with a drill. If only, if only he had acted differently; what then, what then? Would he still be sitting here in this chair, but the world waiting outside subtly transformed; the sound of little feet; the warm light of his homestead? He shook his head to clear the illusion. He doubted it. The world would always be flawed, because the mind as it travelled in time would always find the fault lines, search them out, a geologist to the fissure. He relaxed back in the chair.

But was there a perfectibility on this planet; gardens of Eden hidden like nuggets of crystal in the rock? He suspected so. He still lived for this ideal: his little garden on the prairie.

There were souls who moved through this our world on a golden thread of time, blessed by a separate reality, where shock had not thrown them, rendered them as offering to the god of nightmare – but through this nightmare to be reborn, recast, healed – and even to the end of life clinging to this hope, seeing in it salvation in an afterlife. He shook his head again, but this time at his own ignorance. The simple fact is that he did not know: or he thought he didn't. But what if that strange voice from noises off that called him with its siren message: 'It is all true: and you know it" was right?

Having reached the inner limits of his intellectual circum-navigation, his ideas come round to their beginning again, the serpent devouring its own tail – he sighed, and picking up a paper he idly leafed through it, scanning for something of interest. He tossed it aside in disgust: the same old stories, the same dull preoccupations. What was the point of it all, an endless repetition, an endless series of variations on the theme of life? The only point in the end, he thought, is one's own consciousness and one's own appreciation of it. He supposed food would soon be on the candlelit table outside. He sat looking at the clock as it ticked inside its mahogany case, each stroke the same, yet marking the ultimate separation: time. The door pushed open and the fat man he had seen sitting at the bar came in – he went through to the gentleman's. James hauled himself up and went through into the bar. He purchased half a pint of bitter from the barman. The two players had ceased their game. The billiard table was empty. A party was sat in the French windows beyond. James sank his beer thankful for the refreshment it gave him.

Picking up a cue he rifled a ball across the green baize. It did not go where he had wanted it. He shot again a few times but he was hopelessly off. He replaced the cue and wandered outside. There were more stars out now and the air had a nip to it. It was darker so the diners were more obscure and he saw as he approached his party that the picture he had been enjoying before had vanished in the change of light.

He sat down on the empty chair at the table. Steaming bowls covered the table. His starter sat cold and alone, some lettuce leaves and white cheese. He messed it around with his fork.

"Where have you been?" asked Hermione.

"In the land of Nod," I answered.

She looked at me enigmatically. I tasted some of my lettuce leaf. It had crisp, warm toast beneath it and the cheese was hot and salty goat's. It was rather good soaked in olive oil and enflamed by its balsamic. "We've finished our starters. We're on the main course," said Hermione. So much was obvious. But after his soliloquy of thoughts in the old armchair he was glad of the light relief of inconsequential conversation. "It's very good," he said pointing with his fork at his dish while munching.

"Mine wasn't – wish I'd ordered that," Hermione answered. James had a sudden and uncalled for image of Hermione always ordering the wrong thing. Perhaps that was why she was so thin? But such subtlety of thought he did not communicate to her, restricting himself to: "and what is this main course?"

"I don't know. But its very yummy."

Well there we are, he thought – life reduced to the ultimate banality. Yet maybe that is where eating takes us: back to the nursery. Comfort food. Comfort of strangers. The two women were sitting next to each other next to Madeleine and opposite Withnail Smith. He was well separated from them. Madeleine and Monty were conversing intimately on some subject. He was content to be left on the end on the table with an undemanding Hermione. For the moment.

Day for night. Night for day. The sun setting over Heathrow and stars out in a sky that was both black and blue at once; a shaded garden lit by lanterns, grass no longer green, its colour bleaching into the candlelight. It was an eerie effect – the world caught on its tipping point as it spun from its own celestial candle to enter its dark lawns of starlit void; all the vast vistas of space were revealed in the narrow twilit gap that opened briefly between two worlds, revealing a glimpse of the other, of the precarious, of the cosmic pantheon that sways our dreams as it does the fragile planets.

Things were going quietly around the table. James felt divorced from the two women leant towards each other at the other end of the table conversing quietly but with animated gestures. He smiled at Hermione and she seemed to understand that he would rather be left in quiet contemplation rather than enter into conversation. She nibbled at her food and listened to whatever Madeleine and Montagu were talking about so intimately across the middle of the table. James shifted his chair away from Montagu's annoying bulk, his elbows on the table as he listened to Madeleine, his massive shoulder blocking his view of the rest of the table. He felt listless, tired by the revelatory thoughts he had been having – we can only so long dwell in the cosmic dimensions of the mind without crashing; Icarus; the moth to the flame; the lunatic: like electricity we must earth ourselves or short circuit. The mind must have a stop; he flew again to the moment of stasis, of quietude of the meditation that afternoon: it loomed as a sanctuary – the shed at the bottom of the garden.

James took a large gulp of wine and thus fortified he stood up and wandered off into the garden still restless. Walking towards the flooding butter yellow light of the French windows he heard his voice called. It was Silvanna standing there resplendent in a stylish dark sequined dress. She was made up immaculately so that one could not even tell it: a sure sign of the sophisticate.

"What's up ducky," she said in her thin reedy voice.

He briefly explained his predicament. Silvie inspired confidence; her small dark eyes, her social adeptness, her knowing smile and personal warmth. "Well, you have to choose!" she pronounced. "I'm not sure they know." "Oh don't be silly! What was the fight at the gallery about? Women sense these things anyway." "And men don't?" She looked at him straight in the eye: "No, they usually don't: men are emotionally blind."

"If you say so. I'd better get back to my table."

"From what you say it would be better to stay away. They won't miss you. Come and have a quick drink with me." They sat at the bar and chatted in that lofty old room, its garden scents blowing in the open doors, the creaking of time and echo of so many conversations that must have taken place there, theirs just another to be chalked up by those aged walls. A timeless zone, a sense of drift, and again James felt his head spinning into a pleasant present reverie. Perhaps it also had something to do with the sound of Silvanna's voice, so lulling, so hypnotizing; perhaps her voice was the reason so many confided in her – the cause of her social influence. He didn't mind that, wouldn't let it detract from the pleasant sensation that rendered him one with the room and its warm wood and cream colouring, one with the evening breeze, the soft yellow light, and the hushed tones of the club around.

"You are not listening to a word I am saying," protested Silvanna. Was it that she was unaware of the effect she had on him. He concluded from her petulant expression that it must be. She was beneath her guiles, like a woman unaware of her charms – or simply lacking in imagination, a woman out of her depth. He took pity on her for this, his analysis of her, and stopped his night dreaming and tried to concentrate on what she was on about as she raced off into another long description.

"I am trying to tell you something, interesting," she nudged him; he had drifted away from her conversation again. He blinked, mildly annoyed at this physical intimacy. "Come on, I'll buy you another drink, then you'll concentrate. You see. I was in Katmandu and I was alone. Beano, my husband was in Delhi on business and had left me up there. Anyhow, I met this young man in a bar. He was an Oxford graduate and very shy and restrained. Things were a bit hippyish in Freak Street in those days, and this long haired young Englishman, bearded too, comes up and was really quite nice to talk to. He had these little tablets that we all took with our drinks. I don't know why I did it; it's not like me at all! I think I fancied the bearded one – Beano was very ill and old and I had been looking after him for years, you know. Anyhow, me and this Oxford chappy," this is how Silvanna talked: "walked on out of there. Never saw the bearded chappy again (It was me, it was me, in a previous incarnation – how many bardos have I been thru in this life? – I realized with a thrill, distantly remembering). We wandered off down some streets. I tried to retrace our steps a few days after – but it was no use; we might as well have entered a lost domaine. All I remember is that we ended up in a rice paddy up to our knees in water. There was a flashing sign above a house on the edge of the paddy saying: YOU ARE NOW IN CHINA in large neon red and blue letters. But you know the funny thing; it can't have been, we were a hundred miles short of the Chinese border and we can't have wandered that far. Anyhow we tried to climb out of the paddy but the bank was steep. People helped us I think. I seem to remember we were singing or something. Anyhow, next thing, we were in a horse drawn buggy riding through the centre of Katmandu in the early hours: I suddenly recognized where we were. I told the policeman accompanying us the name of our hotel. I said 'hotel' to him a few times. Finally, as we were approaching the central police station to be arrested no doubt, I had the presence of mind to fish in my pocket. I remember him taking the money. Next thing I remember is waking up in my hotel bed. No idea how I got there."

"I presume the policeman took you."

"Oh, ha ha!"

"But Silvie: it was me. I was the bearded man. That is the extraordinary part of your story: not the story itself." She looked at me in with incomprehension, her eyes narrowing.

"Don't be ridiculous."

"Why did you tell me that particular story?"

"Thought it would be your sort of thing."

"I've known you for over a year. If I told you the year I was in Katmandu and showed you a photo of myself as I was then, you would have to admit I am right. I had forgotten all about that evening; for years I have not given it a thought. But I remember quite clearly going to a small bar off Freak Street one night. My girlfriend had stayed at the hotel and I was unusually alone. A French hippy sold me some pills, more pressed them on me really: 'zey'll mak you zerrry 'igh!'. I had liked the rogue and bought them. Then next to me at the bar I noticed a middle aged woman and a young straight English guy. There were three tabs. The idea just came to me to offer you one each."

"You're making this up," interrupted Silvie, obviously intrigued though still incredulous.

"Was your story made up?"

"No. Of course not. But yours is. You're joshing me!"

"Not at all. I had been travelling around India with my girlfriend for some months." I told Silvie the year it had been.

She counted on her fingers, looked puzzled, then gave a little gasp. "I can tell you what month." I made a quick calculation. She did likewise and gasped again, then looked at me quizzically.

"This is very strange," she said slowly. "There is more to this than meets the eye. I can't believe this, that I should be telling you the story... but no! There's some trick!"

"No trick. More's coming back to me now. I can't remember the Oxford man, he was rather dull with cropped brownish hair, regular features and just very normal. You on the other hand were wearing a wide gold bracelet with a large turquoise set in it. I remember because it was there on a wrist on a hand that you stretched out to take the tabs. I remembered it because my mother had a bracelet like it."

"You are right. I have not seen that bracelet for years. I wonder what became of it? But if this is all true, why did we not recognize each other here in London when we met last year?"

"No hair. No beard," I pointed at myself.

"We only met for a short while, I suppose," said Silvie. "I would like to see that photo of you," she added, "before I am convinced of this."

"Surely. It hangs in my mother's bathroom. We can go there any time."

Silvie sat staring ahead at the wall lost in contemplation. I was beginning to wonder whether I was not imagining the whole thing. Memory wrapped in memory, imagination imprinted on time, imperfect snapshots of the past. Even the fat man I had twice seen that past hour I could not accurately describe, nor the conversations I had had that day. Yet some salient points I could swear to. I could also swear to things I had dreamed of. Did that queer this line of argument? Perhaps it had all been a dream that I had met Silvie at that bar, an imagining fired by her story added to my pensive state? Yet I had been in Katmandu, and had remembered the bracelet...

"There's one thing you are right about," said Silvie coming out of her trance, "that this business of our having met in Katmandu all those years ago, you being the man at the bar, is much stranger than the story."

"It is a better story," I replied.

"Story?"

"Silvie, I don't know. I could be imagining the whole thing."

"A remarkable coincidence then. We were there at the same time!"

"More of a confluence," I replied.

"A what?"

"Just one of my pet theories – how events and thoughts tie in together."

"You are a strange one," she said. "I have people next door. Must go to them. Be in touch. I want to see that photo!" she said, disappearing through the side door by the bar with a wave of her hand.

I sat on a for a few moments wondering, turning the whole thing over in my mind the better to weigh and judge it. But whatever angle I looked at it, it had an odd shape. It was only when I stood up that I realized I was slightly drunk. What was it with Silvie and me and bars? At least there had been no tabs of anything tonight, nor anything slipped into either of our drinks!

I muttered my thanks to the barman and walked back through the French windows and into the dusk of a London night.

The lawn was reeling a bit, tilting with my steps. What had Sylvanna been giving me to drink? Merry, not yet drunk, I determined to drink no more, to sober up – I found the induced lack of self-control annoying. They were still at the table. It had been cleared; a couple of coffee cups signalled where they had arrived at. I squatted down at the end of the table and stared up at the two women. They both looked at him at the same time. Justine was smoking a cigarette. He grinned goofily as though he was ham acting in a hollywood comedy. Justine smiled back. Viki did not: that was her character though, he thought, enigmatic, feelings and motives hidden behind a tapestry, a never ending schema she constructed to smooth her often bruising encounters with the world: in her dreams – they made her position infinitely worse when trying to shift with reality against these dangerous home made designs of hers. Right now Justine was easy to read and that made it easier to relate to her. Inspired partly by his slight state of intoxication he suddenly determined to find out how far they had swapped notes. The recklessness brought on by drinking loosened his tongue and rendered him disinhibited from thinking out consequences.

"What have you two been chatting about, then?" he asked Justine, though Viki might as well have answered into the silence that followed. But she was in no mood to.

"Everything and nothing," Justine answered. She smiled at him, took a puff on her cigarette and blew the smoke out of her mouth sideways so it didn't go near his face. He turned his head above his elbows leant on the table and leaning his chin on his hands looked up at Viki. She looked beautiful and distant, a combination that never failed to disturb him, bring out a latent paranoia in him that he had become an object in her eye, an 'it' as the nasty girl next door had tried to label him when he was a little boy. But just as he felt a familiar rising tide of panic mixed with annoyance surging in him she pushed a scarcely touched panna cotta in his direction, even turned the teaspoon towards him, a gesture of solidarity that had a disproportionate effect on him: giving on the material level was mostly alien to her. Here were two friends then. Either they were privy to each other's affair with him and were at peace (at least superficially) with it; or they were not; and then he wondered if so why not? But then it occurred to him that people often knew much less than one imagined, took the world they encountered at face value; a state of affairs much taken advantage of by brigands and charlatans the world over.

He had been lucky then that his opening remark had not been more liberally addressed. He felt in no state to handle the question answer session that would have undoubtedly ensued a frank disclosure of their state of affairs.

"Must go for a stroll. Need to walk off this booze. See you later?"

They both smiled consent in their own different ways – Justine with a shallow smile and wave of her cigarette; Viki with that wide thin grin that resembled Punch and lit up her face into a sublime state: it never failed, he thought; was it something innate, always there in her, a dormant beatitude of the soul? At that moment of brief intoxication he didn't feel that he was overstating a truth to himself.

James slurred a hurried goodbye to Madeleine and Montagu as he sailed past them; they paid him scant heed, a quick flash of eye contact to register his departure, and then back to their long, ambling chat. What had they been talking about he wondered as he stumbled out into the street?

James

CHAPTER TEN:
THE LONG MARCH 9:25 PM

Out there in the sobering vista of a long London street I realized I was not much drunk after all; the effects of the alcohol had already largely worn away – I should think I had had one too many, no, one more than normal, or something like that. A small engined car grinded from the distance towards me, bouncing on the undulating road surface, leaving a stench of exhaust and deafened ears; I cursed the thing, yet wouldn't have minded having a ride in it. I fingered the car key in my pocket and sagely left it at that and walked north away from my vehicle left parked outside Viki's flat.

Setting a steady pace I padded forward in the London twilight, street lamps glowing against the deep blue evening sky. Soon the ark of the Arts Club lay behind me, a shrinking palace marked in its increasing distance by glowing lamp-posts passed, that as I turned back to look stretched like the bulbs along the upper deck of an ocean liner.

Soon the grander houses gave way to smarter houses of meaner proportion, conceived in the era immediately preceding the Great War in which western civilization (that would be a good idea!) destroyed itself. Already the classical had been subsumed into the suburban – a myth begun on such a high note in the last decades of the nineteenth century with the high art of Pre-Raphaelism and the Arts and Crafts movement; but such high sentiment carried the curse of all bohemia – that the burgeoning middle-classes wanted in, and when they came in their moneyed masses mock tudor and schmaltz was the result, mean and mocking in turn, and massive and all engulfing in its slavery to capitalism, consuming the farm villages of outer London, leaving art itself to deconstructed modernism. The mullioned windows in cheap stone no thicker than a thumb and quaint coach lights wired up from the start to electric. It was the same sentiment which begged for the war which came and destroyed it, which begs for war now, the wars of the small, the mean, the reactionary – of the little power called Britain. There was a crescent cloister of these dwellings that he passed now on his left: for all their vast price the rooms and staircases were cramped, gardens tiny, attics low. They were only desirable for their location. The workers cottages of Chelsea were preferable – but even these had now mostly been rendered into dishonesty by their interiors being opened up into one room mezzanines, as though the owners really only dreamed of living in palaces. The artists and bohemians had colonized Chelsea, money had followed, and a cultural void had now descended on it with a numbing sense of permanence.

Left into Old Brompton Road. The dim antiques shone through the plate glass windows of the row of shops, dimly lit by vague, diffuse night lighting. Opposite a restaurant, its summer awning flapping in the breeze, a few late diners quietly under its shelter like passengers on a ship. A taxi whirred past; in the distance a powerful motorcycle revved up, its thunder echoing briefly, rattling between the street fronts then gone as suddenly as a bee in summer flying fast past one's ear as one lies in the green grass listening...

Flashes of memory as the houses drift past one by one like the trees, bushes, rocks on a river bank. In India, on a road – had I ever travelled it? Hampstead Heath, multiple images – me by the pond with Jonathan; a photo of me and my tiny nephew struggling against a wind. Suffolk – Lavenham in its tranquil beauty; fields; my mother; a harpsichord... and the flashes faded out into indistinct images of our long gone London family house and the colour green, which was the drawing room wilton; green; mud; moss; drizzle; nothing. On my left as I continued down the Old Brompton a garage full of Ferraris and Lamborghinis, striking reds and silvers, long noses smelling the ground, bright steel exhausts promising spitfire performance – these the apogee of craft in a mass produced medium, the pale and useless dream of what had once been promised us all, reserved for the very few so that for them the dream could truly die: to hold is to loose; to drive on empty highways seldom achieved.

And now a right, dodging fast smooth onrushing cars, and onto another of those well to do streets of solid brick housing that positively reeked of prosperity. Inglenook entrances favoured by late Victorians appeared here and there, lending the street a toy town gothic surrealism. Faux balconies abounded; mullioned windows; panelled front doors of heavy wood, large round brass bell pushes and now and then lights on in uncurtained rooms displaying large elegant interiors, all conventional, nothing adventurous. It was as though I was walking through a world of clones, where imagination had been reduced to the obvious, and style consisted of conformity.

After the rather pretty kink at the top of this street a new element was introduced: that of overt commercialism on street level. The large concrete edifices of hotels began to colonize whole blocks here and half blocks there as though some malign lava had flowed over Victorian London and overwhelmed it, wave upon wave, culminating in the squalid backs of the giant glass and concrete hotels ahead up on Cromwell Road. And to serve the clientele of these dormitory palaces were the fast and the fake eateries that infest these types of areas in every modern capital city: branded restaurants with bored looking Asian staff and smelly air vents blowing noisily into the litter strewn alleys behind them – themed English pubs where no local would venture unless perchance to meet a foreign friend or client, or by mistake – and then, for this was still London after all, a sudden hidden gem- a glorious old rooftop crested in wrought ironwork in copy of some French chateau; a famous little restaurant tucked away – a place one might actually care to go and eat in. And then, stumbling by a multi-storey car park and a massive supermarket out onto that great thoroughfare, Cromwell Road, a multi-laned highway that incongruously connected the high baroque residential and retail area of Knightsbridge with that vast waiting room that is Heathrow airport, flowing through the choice streets of South Kensington: an Amazon to the hardwood stands of the forests of houses on its banks.

The traffic streams down the main road, a fast somnambulant trickle: groups of lights stretch into the distance contradicting each other, banks of greens and reds melding together in perspective, their separate distances from me nullified by their brightness, rendering them one large swimming pool of coloured perspective. The traffic obeyed them however, stopping in gathered phalanxes before racing off with a roar into the long stretches, the odd lone wolf car racing by. I cross the lanes gingerly, an alien species on a robotic highway built for machines, taking advantage of the long quiet, empty stretches that by mathematical magic open between the packs of vehicles.

Then in the middle on an island between the streams. Opposite me on the north bank of the river stands the vast rock of a concrete supermarket, windowless, surmounted by a tower of flats. Large precast ramps flow in and out to the multi-storey car parks empty in the night. To either side though of this mountain of concrete , facing the Cromwell Road like the icing cake Venetian palaces that flank the Grand Canal, are rows of stuccoed Victorian residencies that have survived the architectural holocaust around them, bravely defining anoth-er era when aesthetics meant personal delight: now they were covered in garish neon signifying their new status as budget hotels and yet more eateries of hopeless anonymity.

Crossing, plundering north up the side street, I leave the vision of this world behind. I am back amongst the trees, the mighty river left behind. The street before me is empty of people, the huge white houses continuing, turning in from the main road, all joined together in facing rows, intimidat-ing in their massive monolithicism, so different from the gothic revivalism that permeates the more intimate classi-cism of Chelsea. And yet these austere mansions were once too abodes of domestic warmth, palaces perhaps, but fam-ily ones. Now though they were offices or consular depart-ments, or else floors of flats, so many bells on some of their front doors that it was hard to imagine so many apartments clustered so close together in what had been conceived of as a home. The whole leant these streets a dour air, some-what disassociated from the charm of the surrounding area.

The weakness inherent in fear. A dark star is rising. Over this luminous cityscape caught between refined Victoriana and brutalist modern lies a terrible beating heart. It is over there, its epicentre, James waved a hand (a passing stranger might have thought him mentally deranged if there had been one to see), Whitehall, where by the light of the midnight candle the gremlins, sycophants and tawdry power brokers plotted their wars and eco-rape from the dingy offices that lie at the heart of a rotten, broken empire.

Ahead were massive trees: a London square. High in the branches, threading a descant sound of thrill and cold beauty over his thoughts a single bird sang out its evensong in notes of sudden haunting perfection. In the moments of silence that followed James stood still, hoping for a repeat. But there was none. Had it been a nightingale? He didn't know his bird songs but hopefully imagined it might have been: echoes of an old song, half remembered... Here he was, still breathing, and over the borders of the world the sun still shone – and even the grim power purveyors of Westminster could not destroy everything. Cast aside the doom, live on, survive – that most ancient of commands.

The square gardens between the white houses stretched out marginally too narrow for any claim to architectural perfection. The houses were lower and slightly smaller here, so the trees rose to their height, an amply scaled reflection by nature of the human wrought stone-like facades. A lighter touch here then, and the concrete mass of Cromwell Road left behind, so that one was back on a human scale stage set again, that imagined London where other feet in balanced time did tread.

Again there were interiors to peer into. The fashionable German kitchens glinted their silver from spotlit basements, and on eye level ample drawing-rooms reflected their owners' taste, each well and correctly upholstered and hung with the requisite amount of paintings, one after another, until one wondered how much replication, variations on a theme of living this great capital could bear before crumbling into a sea of uniformity.

At the far end of the square ran Gloucester Road. James caught a glimpse of that wide and almost domestic thoroughfare standing empty in the pools of light cast by its street lamps. But he was travelling north. The streets narrowed into alleys of what might once have been a village on the way out of London; or so the winding and intersecting lanes suggested. The houses were more cottages. People appeared again; couples walking, a plump elderly man with a small dog on a lead, a teenager, thin and gangly wearing a self-confident sneer, a small man in an anorak, Pakistani perhaps? A bistro opening warmly onto a cosy corner; then a pedestrian alley between the backs of houses and small gardens. Then this area finished and a more grandiose design took over, similar in style and concept to the Cromwell Road environs, but here untouched by modernity, pure in its brief and more successful in that it ran up to the Park which it fronted as onto an elysian field.

But not yet. He was jumping ahead in his mind. From where he stood at the exit of the alleyway into the street he could not see the park; a congruous row of large white mansions blocked the view a block down from it and block away from him. Here we were back in flat and hotel land again, though discreet, gentlemanly, ladylike, despite the reappearance of the panels of black door bells with their loose trailing wires and dirty lace curtains behind obscure windows. Houses... houses, all framed in the most obvious way – children's drawings in an amateur photographer's frame.

These large white terraces have an almost unreal quality, that of a Victorian stage set of how a provincial might imagine the domestic streets of the great metropolis; a Pol-lock's children's theatre. They stretch up in frill and flounc-es, each side of the street a slab of outsized wedding cake, more cake blocking off each end of the short street so that I was on an island of white fantasy. But turning the corner the end of this fantasy lay in sight: the swaying trees of the Park cut narrowly across the top of the street. The last great mansion had become a smartish hotel, and faced onto Ken-sington Gore, its many balconies and windows peering over the wide road to the trees and lawns stretching up the rising ground beyond. This highway, though as wide as Cromwell Road was nevertheless domestic, tamed by the Park and its grand facing architecture. Cars did not leave London fast this way because the traps of Kensington High Street, Olympia and Hammersmith lay ahead. James stood still for a moment there, savoring the open, green space, decorative iron rail-ings, Kensington Palace nestling in its older, more musty Jacobean proportion amidst the trees, and to his left a modern hotel, but well finished and positioned enough not to grate on the nerves or spoil the whole.

What was that music playing in his head?... a descant voice modulating the chamber songs of the enlightenment, expressing in the romantic tongue sentiment too refined for our brash age to easily grasp: the exquisite rapture of unre-quited love, the loneliness of wandering by night... where had he heard it? – a picture flashed into his head to conjoin with the musical memory. It was recently, yes, that evening he had spent at the Wigmore Hall: there on the stage the sing-er had stood large in his Paul Smith suit and Hugo Boss tie, unremittingly modern in appearance, swaying from side to side with a mannerism that obviously set him at ease. The audience, rapt, was engulfed by the beauty and perfection of his song, which evoked an atmosphere as thick as smoke, an atmosphere that told its own story so the music took the mind off on a fantastical trip. The hall seemed to slip back on the stream of time to a parallel with the period it was constructed: all was perfected in a world of high order in which the authority of the aesthetic vouchsafed a certain solidity, a high cultural imperative that was reflected and embellished by the Edwardian cadences of the intimate architecture of that hall, that last epoch before the nightmare of impermanence descended on humanity with the historical bombshell of the First World War.

And then he thought of her again... so long ago that he had seen her that the image he had of her was as dated as a faded photo from some old album. With a start he understood with that sudden surge of freshness that comes from an idea long submerged knitting together many of our disparate perceptions, that he hadn't realized he was conducting relationships with ghosts; with the ghosts of his imagination; his dialogue not just with the deaf but with those who no longer existed outside his mind: people he had not seen for years, or if he did see, occupied a symbolic perch up there on the shelves of his mind – so many well read books; so many parodies of human kind; so many puppets without strings.

He was walking under the lee of the large glittering modern hotel, an ocean liner moored up on the edge of the Park, the dim understatement of the Palace upstream from it, dully silhouetted through the trees, an ancient symbol of the prowess of a lesser age, a certain orientalism in its proportions. From here the street became strictly commercial, an emporium of shop fronts stretching into the distance ahead. But this he left behind by turning up the hill behind the hotel that led past the Palace and the other vast somnolent mansions with their driveways and staff cottages that dwarfed all sense of propriety in their brash and splendid statement of the high wealth of empire.

119

The slight incline of the hill; hunger; the effects of the drink wearing into a dull sweat as he paced his feet, sore now, one after another as on either side the great houses sailed past, great galleons built to be laden with plundered treasures.

What was it with this succession of figures from the past, all dressed in the garb of another era of my existence on this planet? Even those still in my life – they were not here, on this street, hiding in the gloom under the leafy trees back down the gravelled driveways of the great houses. Here was another one, a massive stuccoed structure looming, a gothic greystokes baroque fantasy built on a fortune dug out of the diamonds of South Africa, a house that would not have been out of place down a mile long driveway; all that was missing were the stable blocks and outbuildings of its country cousins… instead dank bushes crowded its walls, dimly lit by a far off street lamp. A lone walker was coming towards him on the other side of the street, his broad brimmed hat pulled down to hide his eyes as he strode forward purposefully down the hill the way James had come. Now came the end of the lawns that fronted the Palace and he gave it one last glance before it disappeared behind the mansions ahead that lined both sides of the street now up to Notting Hill Gate. In true acknowledgment of the hierarchy that set monarchy so far beyond the reach of New Money, the Palace itself lay rambling and resplendent with its gatehouses, pinnacles. porticoes, staff cottages, garages, workshops, staterooms – no mere money could rival this regal pomp and none could – it was beyond what money could buy, as no doubt its owners intended as its message. In contrast the next mansion was gaudy, a white turreted affair, its gravel neatly raked and shrubbery cut back to a fierce minimalism; it was floodlit, and large vulgar lamp-posts dotted its frontage where were parked up a stable of very expensive cars. Loud brass street number plates unnecessarily shone on its front gates. Cameras whirred on their stalks, controlled by the unseen screen watchers somewhere inside. No, no friends here likely to open a door and shout, Oh James, saw you walking past, come in for a quick drink, do! No naked lover long since dead to his reality was going to call him from one of the darkened front lawns, a siren to his nemesis. He walked on in silence, listening to his own soft footfall, peering at the fantastical houses. But what was it with this thinking of what was not here? Others as symbols of what we are not: brother; friend; mother; lover; enemy; friend – the symbolical structures of our own creation, necessary for us to relate – to what? To ourselves!

The black iron gates that opened onto Notting Hill loomed ahead now. A little wind ruffled the leaf heavy trees. Overhead clouds scudded illuminated orange by the city underglow. The odd star managed a slim quiver through the open velvet patches between the clouds. Somewhere a night bird trilled out cutting the air like a knife, blasting away his thoughts with its shrill melody, as though it was calling out to him: 'here and now. here and now!' It was the second such call he had heard that evening.

Up by the gates now. Ahead the glow and dim roar of traffic of the Bayswater Road. He looked back down the hill he had walked up, its great houses falling back and away, the few street lamps glowing dim, their single bulbs seeming to cast no light beyond themselves, the tarmac glistening black in the dusk – a long black carpet into nothingness.

Yes. The long black carpet into nothingness. That is the past. That is memory. That is the imagination and all its inhabitants. Dwell not there lest like Dante, Virgil lead one by the hand into the inferno. Past, present, future: hell, purgatory, heaven – no! That was too glib. Suddenly tiring of his thoughts he passed through the gates. The doorman called out a cheery "good evening" to him. He called one back. That transaction happily completed he passed on to the main road. Buses, taxis, cars whirred past on their way between the Gate and the West End. A few shop windows were lit to his left. He crossed over and disappeared down a side street. He must hurry. He was late for Maoshan's birthday party!

CHAPTER ELEVEN:
CHEZ CUTHBERT'S 10:10 PM

Cutting through the streets of Notting Hill.

Now he had a purpose he no longer studied the architecture of the buildings on either side of him or the concepts they might arouse in him: rather he passed through the streets adrift in another world, the cityscape but a backdrop now as his mind jumped ahead to Cuthbert's, that loft room he knew so well – it would be lamp-lit and Cuthbert might at this moment be holding a glass pacing his red carpet that would be lit in pools where light fell from another lamp or a ceiling bulb shrouded in a chandelier or held in a bracket, revealing splashes of the disordered paraphernalia that littered that long room, so many testimonials to his long life as a collector of antiques, leaving other parts of the chamber in comparative dull shade. Maoshan would be there already; was she already opening her presents or were they waiting in a pile of coloured wrapped shapes her face all eager anticipation whenever her wide eyes caught sight of them? Suddenly he wanted to be indoors again. He quickened his pace and turned a corner and walked fast, hands in pockets, down the curve of a crescent that bent inexorably towards Portobello Road.

There on the old market street that wound down the hill, a snake through the straight blocks it flowed through, a shop front shed bright light over the black street. James climbed inside and rapid scanned the shelves for a present for Maoshan from amongst the less than suitable merchandise. His eye swept tiredly and somewhat despairingly over dusty biscuit packets, jars of coffee, batteries; then as he scanned on he realized that the shop contained a surprising jumbled array of goods… there were candles, plastic wrapped models of the Tower of London, and oddly, water pistols in lurid oranges, greens and reds – he almost selected one of these, his hand stretching out to take one but his mind rebelling at the inconsequentiality of it as a gift: Maoshan might enjoy it but she might not be grateful; something more celebratory, substantial was wanted. Then he noticed, wedged between some notebooks and an electric kettle a silver bird about eight inches high in a better quality of plastic wrap. He looked at it, her fine beak and elegant plumage, standing on her feet as though surveying all the airs she might fly through. He lifted her expecting the lightness of plastic; but this bird was as heavy as lead. He turned the bird in his hands. There was nothing else like it in the shop. Underneath he found a price sticker. It was more than he expected. It was heavy, resplendent in a repro kind of way. It was just right, somehow perfect. He bought it; the man at the cash desk failed to register any reaction to James's pleasure in having stumbled on the right gift.

Out in the street again. Left at the bank.

Above him in a tree perhaps, came the piercing note of the cry of another bird, as shrill and startling as a warning. For a reason he could not explain a certain chill in the sound of it almost made his heart stop so that he nearly dropped the package he was carrying. He shook himself free of the moment. Startled by a bird! What next?

The doorbell glimmered as he depressed it, as though registering a brief hello, an electrical acknowledgment of his call to the world above. The door buzzed an open. James pushed through and up the steep narrow stairs, past the door of the first floor flat and wound up past books and ornaments that improbably lined the sheer narrow walls until pushing through the heavy curtain he was in Cuthbert's red carpeted, crimson curtained, black walled, long room.

It was not quite true to his image of it, for whatever is? but his imagined interior was dispelled by the brightly lit reality of the hushed room that smelt oddly of new carpet; Maoshan was there, her tiny form swaying next to the bent bulk of Montagu Withnail Smith; Cuthbert was hovering near the kitchen. Cuthbert was the first to spot him, a wry smile livening his thin lips, but Maoshan taking her cue from seeing Cuthbert smile was the first to react. She turned round, grinned all over and pelted across the carpet and flung herself all four limbs off the ground and into James's embrace. They twirled on the spot for a moment like two ballerinas then she dropped to the ground and grabbed the paper bag that held the bird.

"Is this for me?" she asked.

"Careful; it's heavy!"

But it was out of his grasp before Maoshan had absorbed the meaning of what he had said. For a moment the bag dropped precariously: but then the child caught the motion, judging it finally and swung it up in an arc to catch it safely.

"What is it?" she asked.

"Oh, open it my dearest little angel! Do open it! Uncle Monty is so excited!" Monty cried out waddling over, rubbing his hands in not totally artificial glee. He was wearing a purple shirt studded with silver stars, wide flapping trousers and spanish boots beneath – only Monty could have worn such garish garb and got no style grief: his curling black locks dropping below his large white face immediately denouncing the possibility of any criticism. "Open it. open it!" he chanted, dancing around Maoshan like a Russian circus bear.

"Give me room to," she glared. Monty let his arms flap less strongly and slowed his feet until she smiled. Cuthbert, drawn by the performance, was wandering over drying his hands on a dishcloth which he idly tossed aside as he approached us.

She quickly ripped the brown paper bag and exposed the see-through box the bird was in. She peered at it as though trying to work out what it was. Then her eyes grew larger. Monty, Cuthbert and I waited on her in anticipation as to what her reaction might be. She struggled with the plastic that proved tougher to get through than it looked. Cuthbert brought a pair of scissors. Maoshan carefully cut away and exposed the silver bird. There in that light it really looked like something magnificent. Its feet were still entangled in the packaging stand by twists of plastic covered wire. Maoshan with her small fingers slowly unwound them. She lifted the bird. "Now it's free!" she said. She was glowing. "Oh! Thank you James. How did you know it was what I wanted? I have dreamt of having a bird like this!"

I hadn't; and wondered whether she really had. In her young mind had the beauty of the bird as she perceived it prompted her intellect to say and even believe her own assertion? But such thoughts were banished, for Maoshan was on her feet, and the silver bird despite its weight had taken flight. She dived and rolled it, running it down the room making tweeting noises that in her imagination emanated from it, until it stopped, hovering above the birthday cake at the far end of the room with its blown out candles and sliced open centre sitting on a crumb strewn plate.

Montagu looked at me from under his eyebrows, a teasing congratulation playing across his eyes. Cuthbert merely said: "A great success", and moved off towards the cake and Maoshan.

"So how was your party?" I asked the happy girl as the bird landed on the cake rather squashing what remained of it. It rose again bits of icing and chocolate stuck to its feet.

"Wonderful. All my friends came apart from Amber. She was ill."

"And did uncle Monty behave himself?"

"No. He ate all the cake!"

"But there's some left!" Monty protested.

"Would you like a slice?" she turned a sweet smile towards me. I nodded. "But no more for you Monty Greedy!"

"Mount Greed. Not a bad acronym," chuckled Cuthbert. He looked tired and somewhat withdrawn, I thought.

"Poor old Mount Greedy will go to the corner and cry," Montagu wailed, a look of immense sorrow spreading across his features. Maoshan at once relented: "Oh all right. But not too big!"

Needless to say Montagu helped himself to an immense portion and sliced me an altogether meaner one. But Maoshan did not protest. She demanded a small plate for cake with which to feed her bird.

"I do hope your bird is not as greedy as I" said Monty.

"She's not," came the answer.

On the table were the remains of a fowl – their dinner, its

carcass a putrid reminder of our atavistic nature. Maoshan must have noticed my grimace of disgust.

"I didn't eat it. I'm a vegetarian."

"Then why did daddy cook it for you?" I asked.

She shrugged.

"But there's worse," chipped in Monty. "Just this evening Cuthbert told me that the pigeon on the balcony – can you hear it?" he cocked an ear theatrically; and indeed I could just hear a constant cooing. "Well dear Cuthbert wanted the pigeon in question to buzz off. So he took her eggs. Her nest is on the balcony somewhere. Now she will coo fit to drive him mad."

"Serve him right!" Maoshan said severely, her dark brows stuck out like Gandalf's over her flawless white skin.

"So I composed this little ditty to placate Maoshan's wrath," and reaching into the outer pocket of his black jacket Monty fished out a crumpled piece of lined note paper, and he read:

as you ate dead birds
amidst
the heartbreak
of the mother pigeon
and her tragic clucks
as she looked
for her babies
who lay
unborn in their eggs
you had stolen.

Not very good I'm afraid, but all I could manage," he finished, obviously pleased with his effort, closing the note back into his pocket.

"I'll never forgive him," Maoshan glowered.

Sitting there in that long room that I had only a few minutes before borne only in my imagination, watching the lights play in the uncurtained windows, a myriad of different angles of the room displayed, so many different visions of the one room; the ideal form: 'room' – then the kaleidoscope of views of it –

The mother pigeon forgotten Maoshan was back cavorting with the bear form of Montagu, Cuthbert forgiven (for now) was sat watching them through narrow eyes as though capturing the scene as a living memory. It would be her bedtime soon, and Cuthbert would be on his own a brief while before he himself retired, perhaps sitting in the same chair but in a different mood, wondering why her mother showed little interest in her daughter's daily life, a weekend mother and then only some weekends at that. Cuthbert had loved her once, Maoshan's mother: James was sure he had – did such love endure still in some hidden folds and recesses of their lives? James pulled his thoughts from his friend. He sipped the tea he had been given. Maoshan was flying the bird and Monty was pretending not to be able to catch it. So much play. So many roles, feints and thrusts. On so many levels we remain basic to our instincts. And would he have children, he wondered? Another basic instinct to be obeyed? A chore, a worry, a miracle; pure pleasure. All were no doubt true of having a child. But was not Maoshan also his? Were not all children his? And could he bear the intimacy with another woman (or even one he knew) that was so much part of the whole enterprise. Intimacy was what it was all about. It seemed either one lived in brief bursts of being with others or it was a great non-stop blanket intimacy: cut and thrust – instinct. He realized with a start that his aloneness had become valuable to him. He would let fate take care of the issue, he decided. It was not for a mere mortal to decide the relative merits of a life of aloneness or company. Both had their place and time, and more often than not came unlooked for.

♦ ♦ ♦ ♦ ♦ ♦

In my pocket I felt the guilty weight of my mobile. I had felt the thick buzz of its vibrate twice since I had climbed the stairs. I pulled it out and checked the missed calls: Viki 10:19, Justine 10:32. No messages. With a sigh I knew I would call them both back. But in the short interregnum before I did I would allow myself to carry on my gentle reflections not yet wishing to face my two muses… or to think of them.

So there is Maoshan, playing, angelic even as she spirals and with another evasion of Monty's pathetically flailing arms tosses her soft brown shoulder length hair and smiles back triumphant, coquettish even – one can already see the woman in her ready to break out like a butterfly and shed her younger self; yet that too would always be there, present too in the older Maoshan: and she too was aware of all this with that intelligence that is native to all life. Monty would not have made a natural father: his energy was already flagging and even as the girl became more and more excited he was beginning to more fend off her sorties with her silver bird rather than entice and encourage as he had at the beginning of their game. Sweat was trickling down his fat face; it was probably the most exercise he had managed for some time – yet he wore a happy expression of contentment, the child in himself brought out, the same child that was not adult enough to suffer real children for sustained periods.

I felt suddenly guilty for judging my friend Montagu in this way. Who was I to say who would be good at what? People often react in surprising ways: and anyhow – was Monty likely to have a child – no. And how would I be in the role of father?

As if in answer to my question Maoshan walked over to me, her bird suddenly dormant in her hand, dangling dead without her mind's fixation to animate it. Monty was slumped in a chair, his chest heaving, his mouth open. She plonked the bird on the table and looking at me asked: "Did you know you were going to buy me a bird?"

"No. I saw it."

She sat by me and took my large hand and played with my fingers while her face worked as she tried to frame into thought her next question. Her small mouth seemed to take up half her face as it worked in a cartoon like series of grins, suckings in of lips and pouts which latter she managed to do while her pushed out lips travelled from side to side of her face in the most unnatural way. All the while her dark eyes surveyed me. I wondered what was coming. Her little face looked up at me;

"Are you going to have children?"

She was reading my mind: "What do you think?"

"I don't think you will."

"Perhaps I will."

"If you don't, you can always borrow me."

She looked at me with her dark eyes, fixing me with emotion. Scenarios of the future played through my mind like rapid fast forward – skimming clips of illusions. I squeezed her hand and nodded. Had a pact been sealed? As is the way with children her attention was almost immediately elsewhere – but the moment would not be forgotten by her.

Cuthbert was calling her softly, saying wasn't it time for bed. One more game with uncle Monty! Uncle Monty groaned, but a look of resigned willingness affirmed his yes. She trotted off to bait her great bear anew. I stood and stretched, oddly affected by her words. Taking advantage of the hiatus in affairs and to cool my head I opened the small door onto the narrow balcony that looked down on the concrete townscape below, and vertically down onto small green back gardens. All was backs of buildings out here. Behind the townscape rose a semicircle of houses a romanesque church spire counterpointing their Victorian bow backs so I felt I was standing in a virtual amphitheatre.

I flipped my mobile open and it shone luminescent in the dull night momentarily blinding me with the brightness of its screen. He felt his heart beat faster; what was he getting anxious about? That he would have to come off his perch and decide one way or the other? That he would make the wrong decision, an irrevocable decision that he would regret through the long years of the future? That he would lose them both. He felt blind to himself. Unable to be honest because he honestly didn't know. Didn't know anything; not for sure – not even what he really wanted. The mind must stop. Mind: It was like looking at a mirror of the stars instead of the stars themselves. He switched off his thoughts as far as he could, remembering the meditation class: don't follow your thoughts – recalling the bird in the square: "here and now. Here and now." Aldous Huxley had birds who sang that on Island, his idealized psychedelic nirvana community. The light on the mobile screen dimmed. He depressed a key and it blazed out again. Missed calls. Justine. Call. He held the slight wafer of plastic to his ear and Justine's hello was transported through the night to his ear.

Standing there on the balcony perched as a pigeon on a ledge surveying the bowl of mixed Italianate and modern concrete brutalism that so characterized London, James tried to connect with the disembodied voice (unless one can count a mobile as a body).

"Well where did you get to going off like that and not answering your phone?" Her voice sounded oddly high, her Spanish accented English rolling around from high to low.

Was this the start of some sort of proprietorialness of him by her? He hoped not. He was not ready to even think about that yet.

"I walked here; to Notting Hill," he added.

"So you are round the corner."

"Ah: you're at my flat?"

"Of course." Why of course? She could have been any-where. This exchange was beginning to annoy him.

"Are you alone?"

"I'm not with another man if that's what you mean."

Pause.

"Viki didn't ask me on and neither did I her," Justine con-tinued. They must both know. Was his annoyance the coun-terbalance of her submerged anger? He decided to leave it, not knowing, not knowing.

"I'm at the tail end of Monty's goddaughter's birthday dinner. She's being put to bed now."

"Then how about taking me out on the town? I am not in London often, you know."

"I'll be about twenty minutes."

The line went dead in that sudden quiet detachment that is the way of mobiles, and he was holding a glowing piece of plastic in his hand whose function some science fiction writer of half a century before might have been amused to guess the nature of. He was back alone under the stars again but now his mind was in mobile mode, both occupied and entertained with the words and results of multiple calling. He called Viki at her home.

"Hello dear, what happened?" she drawled in a husky voice.

"I'm at Cuthbert's. Maoshan's going to bed. And you?"

"Theo, Hermione and Madeleine came back with me. We're going on to Jaks soon. Shall I put your name on the door?" So they had all gone on without Justine. Had they dropped her? Was that why she had sounded cross?"

"Yes, do please. And can you put plus one."

"Oh. So you are bringing Justine?"

"Yes. Any objection."

"No." But she didn't sound convincing.

He was waiting for the explosion to come. Viki, for Viki, had been most reasonable all day: the oft repeated histrionics relating to herself and the ills of the world had been graciously quiescent. Not that there weren't ills in the world, and Viki's voiced solutions were more radical and intelligent than most, a radicalism James felt was driven by the desperate straights she drove her own life into much of the time. It was not that he didn't sympathize: her life was rendered barely livable mostly – it was truly ghastly for her, but it was within her remit to change all that, only she couldn't – a dreadful catch twenty-two where she was hoist by the petard of her own mental attitude: that could not be changed as it was a whole unto itself. Her extravagance left her poverty stricken; her flat alone, that wonderful loft space built on a raft of debt – her cars which she drove into the ground and replaced with such rapidity; her fads which demanded hi-tech gear that would be her future, that might be her future but just weren't: film and all its paraphernalia; flying; sudden donations to charities – and there he would find her in her loft sobbing like a child that she had no cash and such crushing bills and she couldn't go on. So admirable in intention. And then there was the other strand to her collapses: her psychopathic relations with her father, her only surviving relative. The rows, the betrayals, the reconciliations then the rows again, an endless cycle that deepened in drama each round, until like two punch drunk boxers nearing round ten father and daughter both looked near to ruin. Where this deep familial damage came from James could only hazard guesses: was it genetic or some dreadful deed that passed down the generations, an inflamed scar that neither time nor progeny could heal?

This was her part of the background to the slow severing of their intimacy. If asked why he suffered her as much as he did he would have answered that he felt sorry for her. But the truth might have been else: that he still loved her (but what does love mean? Prince Charles).

What it meant (dear Prince), is that he saw where others might have seen disorder even chaos in her life, a triumph, the victory of the beauty and elevation of her imagination over the sordid details of a reality that kept exploding the myths she lived on. James loved her for the myths, for her vision; and who knows, perhaps she would be proven right, and her vision of reality would come to fruition. About many things she was right, although to the unaware eye it might not appear so.

He was waiting for the explosion to come; when her placid features exploded and the insanity of her eyes was made manifest in a tantrum of such ferocious control that it verged on the psychopathic.

But it hadn't come and didn't come now. Viki finished the call in the soft tones he loved so much: butter wouldn't melt in her mouth. In this instance it would not be unreasonable for her to shout and scream, if such behaviour can ever be said to justify having the epithet reasonable attached to it. And so he went on justifying her furies: the explanations for them always seemed so plausible.

There in the cooling breeze, the heavens turning imperceptibly above the red city haze. Far off a cat yowled; the mother pigeon clucked on in her lost agony. James swept his fingers through his hair and stepped back inside the bright light and warmth of Cuthbert's long room.

Montagu Withnail Smith was stood alone in the room, his fat self placed squarely in front of the hi-fi humming softly an aria to himself. He was looking through one CD after another, discarding each one with an disparaging tut. "Ah here it is," he said aloud.

"Here is what?" asked James.

"Oh! So you are back from your tryst on the balcony with the pigeons. I can't think why Cuthbert roasted bird when he knows his daughter is a vegetarian. He doesn't take her seriously. I as her godfather must have a word with him on this subject, for surely vegetarianism falls under the ambit of God in this context; the sanctity of life, et cetera?"

"I should imagine so, Monty."

"Now the little angel is being put to bed by her single father. Can it be good this parental separation? I don't think it a subject fit for a godfather so I shall venture down that avenue no further. Puccini! We shall listen to Act two. Simply wonderful. But getting the disc into its correct slot and pressing the relevant buttons was beyond the skill of dear Withnail, so I did it for him, and soon we were sitting on easy chairs, sipping small glasses of some vintage port of poor Cuthbert's that no doubt he had been hoarding for some special occasion (he won't mind: Withnail), and listening to the refined and gracious charms of grand bourgeois novecento Italy.

Ensconced thus Withnail felt inspired to expand (in the absence of Cuthbert) on the joys and tribulations of child care. "Are we to hear the joyous squeals of your progeny in this lifetime James, my dear?" I answered that I would scarcely be able to afford to bring up one child let alone fend for a family unless my fortunes changed. "But surely you are soon to inherit?" Monty persisted. Even if that were to be soon it must be cut and shared so many ways it will not make a great difference, I answered. Then I enquired of Monty since we were in the spirit of the thing whether his father had in fact left all to his new wife (so different a creature in her conventionality from his wild free spirit of Monty's mother KarMa, his first wife). "Oh God no!" cried Monty, his purple lips quivering at the thought. "No, no, my boy, all to me! They are not married, you see, not conjoined..."

Monty rattled on but my mind drifted away from his discourse triggered by what he had said. I suddenly realized how my image of Montagu's father was confined and conditioned by just one memory, veiled by drink and time at that; and what's more the image I had held for so long conveyed to me a false surmise of the nature of Monty's familial relationships. On this point, here I allowed my mind to digress in order to follow this train of thought: upon a time I had been in Italy – I was driving towards Rome with my lover and on the radio a song kept playing which contained the words "Rome wasn't built in a day" as its chorus. Nothing very special you may think. And you would be right. But what is interesting is that the words triggered in me the conviction that if our affair didn't work out in Rome we should split up. I don't know why I thought that, but I did. It became what the early French psychologists termed an 'idée fixe'. So when it didn't work out, descended into a morbid series of rows in fact, I drew the conclusion that I had thought to draw, and left her. It was only years later that I out of the blue said 'ah' to myself as the episode rushed back to me: and in a flash I realized that I could have misconstrued the words of the chorus – "Rome wasn't built in a day" could be better taken to mean that a relationship needs building. Yet on that day in Rome I had disposed of what I might have built. So our conceptions can cut two ways, and in that split in the path often lies our fault: lacking the discrimination and rigour to think clearly at the time. Fundamentally I suppose we are lazy creatures even when it comes to matters of the very soul.

The lights in Cuthbert's room swam against the crimson velvet curtains and the heavy Victorian oil paintings shimmered an elegant backdrop to my reverie . . .

It was some time since I had been down to Montagu's father's farm. He was a hunting, shooting and fishing type, a bit of a soak too, left high but not dry by the too many knocks life had dealt him (if the worn look of him was the thing to go by). He was conducting a frail relationship with a rather ill unprepossessing woman the time I travelled up there on a Sunday, though he seemed fond of her. I recalled it vividly as the journey had taken longer than I had supposed and I arrived late for lunch. As I entered there was a certain panic in the old stone farmhouse where the living and dining areas spread open plan under ancient beams from the front door passage. Small windows let in pale squares of white light. It must have been winter. Monty was very pleased to see me. His ersatz mother in law was put out. She had been punishing poor Monty for my lateness. I was told by Monty afterwards that he had drunk the cellar dry "because Christmas is so insufferable, my dear! And so is She!" To belie her ire at this (she professed to being very hard up) he had told her that 'his friend', ergo me, would arrive with a case of fine claret at least. He had mentioned some such thing to me on the phone but weakly and I had forgotten it. They had started without me, all sat round the festive table as they were, although She made a point in letting me know that they had waited long enough. "Where is the wine?" she said to me. I had never met her before. Montagu came to my rescue embarrassed by her. A controversy was quietly frothing between them. But Monty's dad – he was well into his cups by this time and holding forth about this and that; and after a few rapid recovery glasses and a few delicious mouthfuls of lunch rapidly swallowed to catch up with the rest of the table, I fell into countering his rather right wing points – and what is more we both thoroughly enjoyed the sport of completely disagreeing with other; and over cognac and smokes we affably argued until the light in the small square windows faded to grey and then to black and the fire hissed and bubbled in the grate, all the earlier gaucherie forgotten, submerged by the agreeable glow of that afternoon bantering with Monty's father by the fire.

So I now saw how my image of Monty's family life, on his paternal side, was confined and conditioned by this one memory. How little I had known. How wrongly I had guessed.

"Are you with me my boy!" Monty was flapping a pudgy hand in front of my face. "You haven't been listening to my fascinating account of my family history at all, have you?"

"I'm afraid not Monty."

"Off on your own track? Here's Cuthbert back from the angel's bedside!"

"You can go in and say goodnight to her if you want," said Cuthbert quietly.

We both nodded yes and Monty led the way in an exaggerated pantomime parody of treading softly, a finger held up to his lips, a mischievous glint in his eye. I followed more naturally.

Her room was through the heavy curtain and alongside the long room. It was small and her bed was built up to the old window. It was chill in here after the main room. Although her bedside light was on Maoshan was already fast asleep, her breath coming in light pants. Her small mouth a rosebud, her hair splayed over the white pillow like a halo, clutched in her arms a small stuffed animal with a queer expression on its wool face, so as she lay there the lamp shedding a circle of light over her, she suddenly resembled a renaissance painting of the Madonna and child. James smiled at the allusion. Monty was already tiptoeing out of the room. He stayed a moment meditating on the perfect picture and then left Maoshan undisturbed.

It was exactly eleven o'clock when I climbed down the stairs from Cuthbert's with Withnail in tow.

Winding down the staircase and into the street. Monty's heavy clomp behind me. The street strangely silent and grey after the bright lights of Cuthbert's flat; fading like a dream into memory… then the large form of Monty standing beside me, his breathing laboured.

"Where to now? The club?"

"Possibly. We must pick up Justine first. She's waiting at my flat."

"Not on foot? Let's hail a cab!" and with that he flailed his long black cloak over his shoulder so it settled a black shroud reaching nearly to the pavement, and we strode off together towards the Portobello Road to chance our luck on a passing cab.

I cast a sidelong look at Withnail – he glanced away hiding the sly light in his eyes with a supercilious lifting of the corners of his mouth – he did not have the cab fare!

I shrugged inwardly: generous to a fault when he could afford so to be, but impecunious with the casual flippancy a gambler holds towards money – a flippancy that masked a conflicted relationship with the green stuff.

The Portobello stretched empty of traffic either way; neon signs glinting and flashing down its length. We waited some moments for the signature diesel rattle of a cab coasting down the hill towards us; but there was none.

So we walked towards Ladbroke Grove where the traffic flowed both ways from Notting Hill to Harlesden.

Walking with Withnail in tow was so different from walking alone – no longer the somnambulant of my imagination I was become the second fiddle to a Gilbert and Sullivan character – a pirate of Penzance, a wand to his wizardry.

For he cavorted his huge bulk, capering and chattering along the pavement; possibly inspired by the drink he had imbibed at Cuthbert's, or by the prospect of further merriment the night still promised.

On the main thoroughfare the sparse traffic hissed by fast going off up the hill and down past on the other side towards the tube and viaduct – a sort of no man's land between worlds this part of the Groove: behind us the market lands; ahead across the Groove the salubrious housing of Holland Park; likewise up and over the hill – whereas to the north those strange quarters whose names rang with an improbable mixture of suburbia and gang violence: Willesden; Harlesden; Kensal Rise... a peculiarly British mix, where polite 'keep the aspidistra flying' boy scout rectitude lay cheek by jowl with an underworld that passed largely unnoticed by the Great West End.

Finally a yellow 'for hire' light glimmered coming in from the burbs, and as the black cab pulled over its engine ticking over viciously, it burst upon me with full force that I had Justine at the flat and Viki god knows where and I had nothing sorted, even in my own head. Well, it would just have to stay like that, I mumbled to myself as I climbed into the cab behind Montagu.

"Are you all right?" he enquired, craning his outsize head as he settled his ample posterior into the leatherette seat.

"Me? Yes I'm fine. It's you I was concerned about."

"Whatever for? Oh, I see, trying to change the subject; offence best form of defense and all. No. What's all this woman game thing doing to you?"

"I hadn't credited you with as much perception as to have noticed," I replied genuinely.

"Well I have; and I am your friend!" he laid a rather too large sweaty paw on my thigh. I tried not to wriggle away. "I wanna help you."

"But my dear Withnail. I can hardly define the 'problem'. Anyhow, we are drawing near to Justine and in a mo will be with her. Please: discretion." The cab was turning into Campden Hill.

"My dear boy, of course! But I don't want to see you hurt."

"Thanks Monty, thanks," I replied, taking the opportunity to remove his sweaty palm from my leg. I suddenly found his presence annoying. I had to contend with Justine up in the flat and his bulky presence promised only hindrance.

But as I was pondering how politely to get rid of him the cab pulled up and Monty stepped lightly from it and hey presto paid the fare. His relationship with money was beyond me. Like a cat in hush puppies he trod pleated footed ahead of me towards my house door. He was all airy and light, collected of a sudden. Whether he had made this shift because he had registered my concern and now comported himself so as not to annoy was of little import: if he was promising to behave he could come on up.

Struggling through the door; I felt tired all of a sudden. The stairs pulled steeply at my heavy feet. It wasn't the thought of Justine that weighted me as I walked up; rather it was the long day catching up on me – not my normal sort of day by any stretch; not at all. The walls swam in front of my eyes, the horrid floral patterns of the communal stairwell becoming almost pretty, decorative. Withnail was somewhere behind me labouring his bulk upwards. I stilled myself a moment. My heart was beating too fast; a thin film of sweat had broken across my forehead. Justine... how could it be the thought of her, that goddess, who assailed my body through

my mind? The day span through my mind, a rapid kaleidoscope of composite images, some real, some less so – splintered reformations from the inaccuracy of memory. Viki's
legs naked in her flat, a shock of her blonde hair; Justine in
the car, in the sun, in the shadow driving in from Heathrow.
The Arts club with its fairy lighted garden; the long trudge
to Notting Hill past formless blocks of monolithic buildings;
Cuthbert clucking forth in his high pitched voice as he propelled himself nervously about the flat, holding court. It was
already a dream, already gone: and yet he would now have to
play out the consequences upstairs, later with Viki too; consequences of events that had already slipped into the past and
lost their immediate meaning – so many interpretations, so
many jostling scripts vying for authenticity – an authenticity
they could only achieve by forcing or persuading another to
accept them. Sins of the ego.

"Are you going to move or not? I thought I was the slow
one!" Withnail's voice boomed behind him. He felt his heaving presence close, and moving on up the stairs rang his own
door bell partly to save looking in his pockets for his latch
key; partly to forewarn Justine of their entrance to his flat.

Opening the door he passed through the narrow corridor
that served as an entrance lobby and through to the large back
sitting room from which issued a fog of smoke. Justine was
sitting on the floor her face softly illuminated by the dimmed
lighting. She glanced up from what she was doing – sorting
through a stack of CD's. A half rolled cigarette was on the low
glass coffee table in front of her and a scatter of open magazines to one side – a soft blues track trickled from the speak-
ers – News 24 played silently from the TV behind her. "Made
yourself at home," he said inadvertently and ill advisedly.

"What do you expect when you leave me with your
friends!" her heavy accent on this last word left it open to

several meanings, none of them good. It felt as though she was about to embark upon one, but the shadow of Montagu Withnail Smith hove into the doorway, and as he slipped his bulk gingerly through the narrow aperture Justine shut up. Her scene, if that is what it was going to have been, was for James's ears only.

"So we're going to Jaks," she addressed Withnail from the floor; more a statement than a question.

"Yes. I suppose we are," he replied. "But first," he continued, rubbing his hands together like a little boy inviting them to the sweet shop: "Let's go to number 99 Church Street, just round the corner, where there is a very nice gathering of wild young people, or so I hear."

"Young people! What in the world are they?" said Justine. Her curly black hair fell in ringlets over her olive skinned face, her large brown eyes sparkled with the light of the candle on the glass table.

"Well, let's call them just 'wild' people then," Montagu replied somewhat impatiently.

"My friends!" James through his hands up in mock sympathy. Both Monty and Justine smiled: some ice was broken.

Enough to carry on with.

Now there was a triangular tension firing round the room. Was Withnail going to play ball boy while James and Justine played hide and seek with her ball of knowledge about Viki? They all stood there wondering for a moment as the ice cracked and thawed enough for it to be apparent that Monty was a player: the ball would not be dropped. They all perceptibly relaxed. A warm evening breeze rustled the curtains. Out in the street a car honked briefly. The cat walked in mewing. "I'd better feed her," said James.

He walked through to the kitchen its narrow window black onto Campden Hill. He flicked on the light and shadows leapt into the brightness, and in the window was reflected back at him a dimmer illumination of the room he was standing in. He pulled the cat food tin from the fridge and peeling its red rubber top smelt the familiar odor like corned beef, old socks, a dreadful claret vintage. He wondered that Mini should eat it – but no doubt the offal merchants had employed the correct balance of nutritionist and taste bud analyst to both feed and tempt the cat. Sometimes she left if, others gingerly seized small chunks of the jellied matter. Now she mewed anew as he scraped her plastic bowl onto the floor and she went to it with studied attention. He stroked her back once and her tail swept up. A quick purr. Then she set to. He left her there, small munching noises, and switched the light off leaving the door ajar, her faint form silhouetted now, more guessed at than visible.

The thought crossed his mind that perhaps he should just confront Justine. Did she know that he had had sex with two women that day, and dined with both of them together? But how to put it? And Monty was there and was keeping mum. No. It wouldn't do. Let it play out.

The music came to an end. Justine sat moodily on the floor inhaling deeply and blowing out vapourous plumes of smoke so she looked like the gipsy lady on the Gitanes pack, a classical sculptural form rendered sensuous by the wide plumes of smoke, a counterpart upside down in the air of her flounced dress. 'Flouncing up and flouncing down', thought James to himself as he watched the scene from the door unobserved on his return from feeding the cat. Monty was pacing, his face down, wrapped in some trivial preoccupation. He watched the still smoke wreathed figure as she sat; suddenly it was hard to remember their passion of only hours before. Then as his mind remembered their love making he felt aroused, and he searched her body for confirmation that it was the same that had entwined naked in his arms. But without the touch, the affirmation of naked encounter, it was history already – and he felt a rising panic that he might never experience Justine like that again, that she would forever remain a dressed and distant self; that intimacy would never again be found or reinforced. He wondered at his panic – are we never satisfied: must the mind always jump to the next moment as a problem simply because the previous one had been solved? Then he thought of Viki. He thought of the two of them, together. No! Stop! That was purest fantasy. Then, with a hot flush of annoyance, his mind forgetting this unlikely erotic scenario as quickly as it had imagined it, he glared at Monty pacing his carpet so idiotically, bulkily, vacantly, and with a great deep wish wanted him to vanish so he could seize Justine in his arms and sate his lust.

As though sensing the power of his thought Monty looked up and smiled hesitantly, brushing his hair back nervously with one hand. Alerted by this gesture Justine glanced up and surveyed them both in a rapid sweep of her dark eyes. "Is it time to go then?" she said, stubbing out her cigarette.

CHAPTER TWELVE:
THE PARTY 11:11PM

They elected to walk as it was hardly far to Church Street. Up the brief steep hill and left onto Campden Hill, three abreast, then Monty a pace or two behind as the pavement was narrow and cluttered with posts. The air was moist and slightly chill now. Their footsteps echoed alone in London for a moment, until a car roaring up the Hill drowned them out. When they came out on the Hill it was deserted and quiet, the tail lights of the car disappearing south as the road fell between the leafy trees that ran towards the park.

The leafy trees swaying quietly above his head; the soft murmur of distant traffic, as soothing in that moment to his mind as the torrent of a far off river; the clarity lent by the night to individual noises – a door slamming here, a voice calling there, a gust of wind playing across the cables overhead – all this set James into a reflective mood. He let Withnail who had been pushing up behind them get ahead of him, then lagged back so Justine and Withnail were now walking ahead together. The soft airs of London washed over him, a balm to his depleted senses. He needed replenishing. This decision. This decision hovering over him, if decision it was – more conundrum; what to do? He shook his head. Only a jumble of images came to him, from the past and future, imagined and actual, intertwining and weaving an impossible tapestry of shifting shapes and forms, a kaleidoscopic out of focus movie of which he was the involuntary director. Was this internal movie his life, his fate, or just his flawed vision. He had no idea. Whatever was going to happen to him was going to happen whatever. Of that alone he felt sure. He felt adrift, a fish in a multitude of sea currents being swept blindly forward. And his future. What had been decided? Which woman? Either? Neither? Did it even matter? "I don't know the verdict!" he half cried aloud. Justine turned her head as she walked alongside Monty. But she was too far ahead to have heard what he had never intended to say out loud. Be still the images, still the mind, he said to himself as though lecturing to a madman.

Still the mind, still the mind. Outside trees swaying in the evening breeze. The large sloping shoulders of Monty heaving step by step away from him, flanked by the slim waist and wide hips of Justine, her long black hair flowing in curls from the height of Monty's massive shoulder. Two silhouettes disappearing ahead in the night and I feel, I feel held back as though in a dream, some force of gravity weighing my steps so I can never catch them up. Stuck in an eternal movement of trying hopelessly to narrow the space between myself and my destination: two universes held apart by gravitational thrust. And inside, inside this my universe, from where the trees and Monty and Justine are seen, observed, computed, is this idea of them being computed then also just another of the myriad of forces and images vying in a weird gestalt of visions, jostling for prominence. I see my mother floating past me in the garden on a summer's day wearing her battered pink straw hat; a photo of my grandmother whom I can scarcely remember; my grandfather, an austere photograph of a man I had never met but knew from so many different photographed angles. Visits to his country house, now a museum; his walking cane, still in my possession, his features, reflected in my own. Visions of clouds drifting white against blue, clearer in my mind's eye than the outer world of night I am passing through: an introversion deeper than thought – for the nakedness of the vision is more vital, more poignant than thought. And unless I were to stub my toe to be thrust into the external world while I walked trailing behind my friends in this now deeper somnambulance, that too had become less real than the fireworks of my inner vision. I let great patterns of colour swirl across my retina. I stopped and stood still to allow the colours and light to gather in intensity. Great floral patterned explosions, purples turning into greens, reds, luminous white expanding around its rims like a Rothko painting; patterns weaving, coalescing, changing. But the very act of standing still had been the metaphorical toe stub. I felt myself standing there more concrete and the swirl of imagery lost its intensity. I opened my eyes.

"What is the matter James?" Justine was crying out, starting back towards me, her mouth agape.

"Are you all right?" Monty echoed, his stentorian voice booming between the low terraced cottages of this long narrow street.

I looked up at the leaves of the small trees playing in the wind above me. I felt the breeze brush my face. Up in the sky a jet liner was cruising down over towards the west: Heathrow. It felt good to be alive.

"You day dreamer," said Monty taking me by the arm.

"Night dreamer, more like," Justine said oddly as she took my other arm.

"I'm okay!" I said pulling away from them. I wanted the freedom of the street, to feel the airs again, to feel just me and the world with nothing between us – not even any thoughts!

Now I was the one to walk ahead as they walked together falling back into whatever conversation they had been having before they had noticed my absence, my reverie.

At its bottom the street opened onto Church Street, a thoroughfare that somehow retained its village like quality of low shops, gardens and small houses. I led the way across the road and walked on down to the familiar blue door next to the bakery.

Curtains billowed red and blue from the tall windows above the shop; people in fancy dress were sitting out on the sills; the door was wide open and more fancy dressed folk were scattered down the narrow corridor adorned by feathers and coloured lights, and on up to the bend in the stairs the house was crammed with people. A man not in fancy dress pushed past them out of the house as they stood there hesitantly on the doorstep looking in at the smoky scene. Music trickled thinly down the stairs and from the open windows.

"Go on! Take the plunge!" the man said.

James peered at him as though he were an apparition. His face was white as powder in which large brown eyes swam as James stood there captured for the moment – he may not have been wearing fancy dress but that made him seem to James all the more strange: his sensual lips; his youth; his height –

a kind of wild decadence seemed to emanate from him: his features were mobile and in his eyes James suddenly felt he could see his inner world, a world of colour and vision, excitement and happenings, as though he were living now, not merely observing – a state in which the inner had become the outer, the two were fused, and here embodied before him was an example of tantric bliss, of embodied unity and instant experience. James stretched out a hand and began to move his lips. "Go on!" the man said. And it was as though he knew James, knew his limitations, and was lightly mocking him, daring him. James felt a thrill sweep through him. The man was walking away down the street on his long legs, an aura of possibilities around him. James took a few faltering steps after him. Then realized he would not know what to say if he caught up with him.

"Probably high on drugs," Monty said coming to his side.

"Probably," James replied.

The others disappeared into the house. James stood a few paces from the open doorway. Down the hill the man was still visible, small now, disappearing. James watched as the figure shrunk and held onto the feeling that had come over him. It is my feeling, it belongs to me, he said to himself. If only I can become like him. But what was this secret enigma, this sudden passion for realization that had awoken in him?

The street was empty now. He turned to the door and went hopefully inside – hopeful that the man's aura lingered on inside, and maybe had infected others there, his friends, someone.

The staircase was crammed with people sitting, talking, smoking, drinking, laughing, gazing, pushing up, pushing down: it was as though the small house had been transformed into a pirate ship full of boarding crews. There was no point in trying to hurry up. James found himself engaged in minute conversations with people as he found himself face to face with them in the crush. Unexpectedly he kept finding traces of the tantric man in the people he passed, as though they were all members of the same family. It might have been the fancy dress, the youth of the crowd, some infectious gaiety – but as he climbed higher up the stairs, winding past the first floor of party rooms decked out in great drapes like bedouin tents or the sails of a ship, lit from behind, the atmosphere of unreality increased as did his excitement. At the top of the house he went into the front room which was empty enough for people to be dancing. He went to one of the windows. Church Street was all quiet below as though unaware of this secret world behind its walls; directly beneath he saw the tops of heads peering out from the floor below. In the room a large man dressed as a Red Indian was dancing. Three girls were dancing about him. He was immediately struck by their beauty. To see one beauty is special but three together extraordinary. The Red Indian seemed to be ignoring them as they writhed around him. Their eyes were on his every movement: he had an easy grace about him which suggested he knew his power. If anything he was better looking than they. He caught James's eye and smiled as though he knew him. James felt flooded by a happy warmth that he could not explain to himself. He wandered down to the first floor and there in the front room below the one with the Red Indian were teenagers all over a four poster bed passing joints. Jimi Hendrix was playing loudly. Couples were snogging on the floor. He was about to retreat when a voice called out: "James, we're over here James. Come and join us!"

Under the tall window was a table with a crowd sat on a wall bench and odd assortment of chairs. James squinted through the smoke and colours to make out who had called. On a large wing backed chair up against the window sat the most extraordinary figure of a lady. She wore a high tiara and long white cloaks and her face was animated to the extreme. Rather like the Red Indian upstairs her crew gravitated around her. She looked in his direction, smiled and beckoned to him. James began picking his way across the bodies on the floor that lay between himself and the table, muttering the odd 'sorry' as he misplaced his feet. There at the table were Justine and Monty, also Madeleine was sat squeezed into a corner near the window on the banquette looking uncomfortable; she smiled weakly at him and waved a small hand mouthing something – but what it was he could not hear through the music. Dulcie was sat on a chair a vague smile on her lips and a large glass of booze in one hand: she did not notice him. And even through the Hendrix he could hear the thin, nasal whine of Mo's voice – James located the back of Mo Mogul's head, saw his waving arms: he had obviously found a willing victim in the shape of a bored looking pudgy white man to listen to his ongoing diatribe about his Bangladeshi homeland and its relationship to 'Britishness'. The grande dame in the tiara beckoned him on as he faltered, and waved imperiously to the people on the banquette to budge up. James squeezed in and sat down the open window looming over him, the night dark above the houses opposite, as he wondered what he had let himself in for.

"So you're the writer?" she said turning the full force of her personality on him.

James smiled and was about to reply when the woman lost interest him having captured him, and turned her attention to a presentable middle-aged man sat next to her dressed in a well cut suit and shabby tie. James felt adrift for a moment; then he found Mo's thin voice cutting into his attention: "Hitler was right you know," Mo was ranting, refilling his wine glass as he went on. "Only except he did not like coloured people.

Why was that? I don't know, I don't know... " he trailed off in a disappointed voice. James could not hear his victim's reply. Mo when drunk was ludicrous. "Hitler was a great man but he hated us!" Mo wailed on unstoppable now. He was somehow saved from opprobrium by the patent absurdity of his position. Or perhaps it was the mad drunken look that had taken over his drunk black eyes, normally so sharp and intelligent. Mo when sober noticed everything that was going on, even behind his back. What drove Mo to these depths, transformed his quick subtle nature? Strange how this inner process proceeded, James thought as he looked at his friend Mohammed Mogul, sitting, swaying more like, in rhythm to his insane incantations rather akin to the Jews swaying at the wailing wall – strange in so many ways: where it came from; why it happened; what inspired it? What is this madness that grips the human race? Is it of the mind? – a series of jumbled images and the best the poor mind can do is turn them into some sort of pattern, any sort of pattern – as long as it makes sense to the mind, even in its most addled state.

So now sitting there the banal conversations straggling ridiculously about my ears; the smoke filled room; the Hendrix still rocking on thirty years after his demise – and these kids into him again as though he was their very own youth rebel: I couldn't help thinking something had to give – the world was about to throw out this old paradigm born as it was from an age of political ineptness and natural catastrophe that was fast melding together to form the cataclysm that would necessitate the change.

But meantime the party was rolling on with no thought of the morrow.

"Stop being a bore, Mo!" Clara drawled an imperiously languid admonishment from the end of the table where she was still ignoring James sat next to her. Mo ignored her remark so set was he on his saga which had now moved on to the praising of Winston Churchill to his sweating victim. Emily, her daughter, a simulacrum of her mother only elevated from her slight vulgarity by the extreme beauty of her youth: though signs of her mother's ruthlessness with men could already be discerned in the way she brushed aside her admirers advances with wonderful coldness – Emily danced into the room followed by a troop of admirers.

She was pretty, she was daring, clever and ruthless: all was writ large on her face and in her body; beguiling too with her wise regard which when it fell on you made you feel the most important man alive – so James found as her smile fell on him. But her eyes soon moved on and he was left by her as alone as her mother left him by her side. "Quelle femmes fatales!" Madeleine picking up on his emotions said to him.

And with her merry troop of followers in tow she spun about the room, disturbing the bodies on the floor and on the bed until all the room was in commotion. Hendrix was singing Purple Haze. Then she clapped her hands:

"The bus to Jaks is downstairs!" she cried out.

And sure enough from outside the window James heard a commotion of voices. Leaning out of the window he saw a large double decker bus, the old Routemaster with its open back platform with "for private hire" posted on its front. Fancy dressers were already climbing aboard with a hilarity absent from most bus stops; some were clutching bottles, holding half full glasses, others climbing aboard in threes, arm in arm, some singing, some already climbing off again.

A general move was being made out of the room, out of the house.

"Are you coming?" James asked Madeleine.

"On that there bus?" Madeleine drawled in her drawliest drawl.

155

"Well its a free lift to Jaks and it looks fun. How else are we going to get there?"

"Not my kind of fun, all these drunken twenty-somethings. I'll take a cab. Care to join me?"

"No thanks. It looks my kind of fun, a double decker full of fruitcases cruising the London night."

"Each to his own!" Madeleine stifled a yawn. She looked pale and tired, drawn almost.

"Anyway, I thought you had gone straight on to Jaks with Theo and Hermione?"

"And Viki!" she reposted. "I thought I'd drop in and see Clara and Emily for a while – But what's going on between you two is none of my business!" she gave me one of her ruffled conspiratorial looks. "But James, you must decide, Its only fair on Viki – she looked quite upset after you left the Arts Club. So did Justine."

"Yes! What did happen after I left, between them?" said James quickly, taking his chance. But Madeleine having proffered her advice had now moved on in her mind as her eyes were already scouring the street looking for the yellow light of a passing cab.

Monty's large figure came dancing up before them, his long cloak billowing, a smile playing across his face. "What fun this all is!" he said. In tow behind him was Justine. "Where have you bin, James?" she said coming up to him her accent thick with emotion.

He was about to try and explain when Emily appeared and began orchestrating a general move onto the bus. Justine followed James closely up the narrow winding stair to the upper deck.

The bus drove off more like a car, following its own nose, diving up sidestreets and short cuts. When it stopped at a light or a pedestrian crossing late night revelers on their way home or inquisitive types engaged in banter with the ever changing company that thronged the open rear platform. Some even climbed on and joined the party. Others climbed off again at the next stop, one shouting: "fucking weirdos!" drunk as he was as he leapt off the platform into the dim night.

Justine was sat alone at the front of the top deck staring out of the window as though she were on a normal bus trip. Something seemed to have made her more solid; her usual Latin vigour dispersed. James felt a wave of panic akin to guilt – was it due to him: he supposed her brief London sojourn had been a dark trial in a way; but he saw little he could have done about it. If he had been someone else he would of course have acted differently. But he wasn't, and if time were played again he would surely have forgotten his past future and repeated exactly the same moves. It is only after an event that we slowly and often painfully learn.

And now he saw little he could do about it. He was still trapped in the same now of unknowing about the future. Was this the source of his rising sense of panic. He could go up to her and sitting next to her hug her, warm her back to life. But then she would, holding him responsible for her state rather than herself, cold shoulder him – and could his warmth melt through that. It was worth a try, he thought: always put love first (in the most charitable interpretation of that word).

looking down through the conductor's mirror at the revelers hanging off the white poles of the platform below, swinging like porn flick girls as the bus cornered and swung feeling fast, very fast, at thirty; beginning to pace through the party of the upper deck, the nape of her neck appearing and disappearing as he swung with the bus from grab to grab, his view blocked by chattering people – and that was the difference between this and other bus rides: everyone was talking, exchanging, laughing: did humans have to be made part of a party before they were brought together; why so distant normally when after all we are all related? But this small reverie was never concluded since he felt his arm grabbed and looking down saw a drunken Mo glaring up at him through rheumy eyes, a flashing lop sided smile enlightening his face.

"James! How're you doin'! Why Emily's mother not coming?"

"I didn't know she wasn't," I answered.

Mo kept a firm grip on my arm. "Why Clara not come? Was it something I said upstairs at the table? Did I say wrong thing?" Mo went on in his heavy accent.

"No. I'm sure not," I replied, eager to catch Justine while the moment was still alive, her there alone on the front bench in that mood.

"Good; you are sure? Good." He momentarily tightened his grip on my arm then let go. I moved off with a perfunctory gesture as the bus swung in a wide arc. Outside focusing through the window reflection of the party on the upper deck, I could see Hyde park corner flow slowly past, its vast grand buildings and monuments beached amidst the traffic flow. James lurched with the bus and finally neared the front and discovered an unimpeded view of the nape of Justine's neck. Had he read her mood correctly? Sat there like that, so still, faced away: what was her mood? Quiet happiness? He guessed not.

He perched next to her on the quarter of the banquette she had left free. She moved aside without averting her gaze from the straight ahead. He sat in comfortably next to her, the swaying of the bus restful now sat. Justine seemed to be wrapped in contemplation of the unfolding scene displayed before and below her through the plate glass flat front window, so close up. He remembered she had not seen London before: an explanation?

But glancing at her she seemed far away as though sat on a distant beach staring at a mysterious sunset. He wanted to reach out to her but didn't know how. But in that sunset land, on that beach, sitting there, the waves pounding – then he knew. He knew it all as he watched the sun sink a red orb into the swollen ocean. It was with her his future lay, his now crashing through into the present moment. The sun set. The world was plunged into darkness. James opened his eyes. He was still on the bus, swaying; he lurched forward and sat next to her. She snuggled up to him and fitted into his arm as though she had always been there.

Suddenly he felt tired. Tired of the whole panoply of events that made up the inebriated whirl of London life. He wanted to sleep there. Sleep in her arms forever. His skin was grey with fatigue and his eyes stung red and for a moment he closed them as though he could grab a cat nap. But the leviathan bus bumped to a halt finally beached on the curb of a narrow lane in Charring Cross. Everyone was running out into the cobbled back street with its bolted garage doors and back doors of restaurants. Over one of the back doors was a ragged awning underneath which stood a polite looking bouncer and a small queue of hopefuls behind the inevitable rope. 'Jaks' was emblazoned in worn red neon above the door.

James

CHAPTER THIRTEEN: JAKS 12:11AM

Justine leapt to her feet and smiled fresh and loving at him. James felt so leaden he could hardly move. A reserve of energy must be summoned. Out on the street the fancy dressers were playing as they came off the bus like so many children at a party by a lake in the lost domain… wipe the tiredness from eyes; Justine's warmth of smile irradiating me but failing to lift the fatigue. Inner happiness and relief flooding through with realization. New reality. Second wind summoned. To feet, heavily. Feels as though bus still swaying. Justine ahead her head disappearing a fuzz of high hair bouncing down the spiral stair. Last one up here. Glimpse of Monty on street strutting and cavorting, long cape billowing though no wind. Strange that. Is it the magnetic force of his prostrations that forces the cloth to flow – some strange priestly resonance. Onlookers were clapping; Monty mock bowed the applause. Mo stumbled up to him and tried to drunken hug him but Monty must have side stepped for Mo fell on his behind and looked up startled for a moment before breaking out into a smirking giggle. James stood there watching alone from the upper deck of the bus. The doorman swung the rope aside to let the party through into Jaks, to the annoyance of those in the queue who were still corralled along the grey wall, a sad small line up the pavement. And then there was Justine, all grace and energy as she moved towards the entrance. A cab pulled up. It was Madeleine. Out of the cab climbed after her Hermione, Dulcie, Jimmy Rafael and Theo, fat and prima donnaish as usual; and last but not least, Viki.

She was dressed as though for the gym and she was not smiling. She barged forward through the now throng at the door and pushed on through without seeming to notice the bus, just a bus, standing there.

James groaned inwardly. Now he was sure he would have to confront Viki, or avoid her: avoid her would be easier. What was there now to say? Nothing. Suddenly Justine had assumed centre stage of his universe – magically almost, as though by osmosis, her presence seeping and looming until there she was, the full grown genie sprung from the bottle. And Viki… his heart lurched… what to do? Don't think, don't think, don't think, chimed the mantra in his head like the tolling of a great bell. Ignore and it will go away. And it must go away. Justine was the future. With Viki there was too much past. Glimpses of moments flashed past his mind's eye like so many stills from a DVD scene selection. The time when she was balling in a park and it was cold and he was worn to nothing, about what he could not recall. Viki smashing things around the house, kicking with her great feet. The pity he felt for her. A mean gesture. It spun round and came round, a kaleidoscopic myriad of too many details that did not add up. Why should they add up? he thought to himself. After all one could carry on in the same bardo forever – and ever, and ever! Aye; there's the rub. Indeed. But there was more to this situation than jettisoning the past, or moving on, or whatever other banality one might wish to apply to it. It was as though the future had opened up and like a great maw was inexorably sucking him on and in. Time had its own gravity: and now events were spun in motion he was being sucked into a vortex he could no longer deny. And so. and so… it was all inevitable, in a sense, already written, devoid of responsibility. Justine was his.

Finally he moved down the double decker towards the spiral staircase. Outside everyone had gone on in to Jaks, apart that is from the forlorn queue of hopefuls still behind their rope.

The alleyway opposite, grey and damp, shrouded in shadow, housed a crumpled figure dressed in rags and lying on cardboard, only a glistening white face illuminated brightly by the sickly cast of a streetlamp that lit up the entrance of the alley a fluorescent triangle cut off abruptly at an angle by a wall so the rest of that cul de sac was obscured. James walked over slowly drawn by an impulse he could not locate. The figure was sleeping. A soft smile played over the sleeper's lips as though she was having a sweet dream. For a moment he stood there captured by a feeling of peace that perhaps emanated from the tableau before him; and to his mind came some words the meditation teacher had spoken that afternoon: "… take care to address even the meanest beggar with respect – masters walk under many guises… ." He stood there lost in a timeless silence, the neon sign above

Jaks flashing the seconds, a semaphore to his stasis. Then, inexorably, he felt himself drawn back into the world, slipping back into the stream of distractions around him – a car passing, a shout from down the street, a cold gust of wind sweeping dust in swirls along the pavement and up into his eyes. A shout brought him fully to his senses:

"James! Hoi! What you doing standing there!?"

The large figure of Monty stood looming in its billowing cloak on the opposite pavement next to Jaks entrance, and next to him stood the smaller figure of Madeleine.

"We came to get you!" Bawled Monty.

James crossed over to them not looking back at the apparition still sleeping in the alley entrance.

"Aren't you comin' down?" drawled Madeleine; "or is there something else stopping you?"

James felt a tug at his heartstrings at her remark; but he gritted his teeth and walking on past his two friends went into Jaks.

Along the corridor. Dim; cheap carpet beneath feet. Visions of hands and arms coming out through walls to grab me. Head spinning slightly: what from? The vision of the tramp – Virgin Mary? – the two women downstairs now, Viki, Justine... sound coming up the stairs now, thumping, voices raised; smell of smoke. Cloakroom girl in her little box on corner (what a job) – hand her coat. Lighter now, slight spring in step as gingerly step by step go down narrow double back stairs and through doors and into the red light of many people thronging around. Friends at large table, some of them I can see: Theo, Hermione, Jerry Rafferty, Mo, others too not know well or at all. At glistening bar Viki sat like a great toad on barstool, face jutted forward to dominate, glaring. Alone. Justine? Scan crowd, cannot see her. Need drink. Bar first then. Near Viki but not too, for fear... of what? Nagging anxiety clawing at stomach again. Drink will settle that. Too much of a drinking day today: tomorrow none; a day of atonement, of sitting down to work and business chores too; always more and more of those piling up in this our contemporary metropolis. Elbows land on bar perilously near Viki. Bartender ignores me. So does Viki. Under the dragon's gaze.

The dragon looks up at me as though catching sight of me although she must have been aware that I was there from the instant of my arrival – perhaps not? Who cares? Who knows? She knows. Each of us trapped in our own little bubble of consciousness, so isolated, so fragile. Her eyes are glazed as though she is consciously turning me into an object. A condescending sneer informs her lips, subtly. I sit up on the nearest barstool. I twist slightly and attempt a grin in her direction but feel it manifest as the sneer of a cowering dog. Wonder if looks like that to her? or is it just me? my internal interpretation of the signals my body might be giving out. The music deadens any need for idle conversation between us. I resist an urge to shout. What. What would I shout? That I find you intolerable; that the feelings between us are too resurrected to be alive; that I can't take it any more? None of this is worth shouting. We keep up our game of masks, hers hardening so slightly. Then in a surge of action she is gone. Her place vacant; like the dart of a lizard into the night.

"Yes sir? Drink sir?" the barman butts in with impeccable lack of sensitivity. I nod. "Vodka martini, please."

I sip the bitter drink vacantly. Faces swirl anonymously through the gloom, occasionally a face with all its human features caught in a flash as it stops, frozen in time by one of the thin spot beams. None I recognize in the swirl of the floor space around the crescent shaped bar. The table seating my acquaintances is hidden by pillars and a low balustrade. Suddenly gripped in the stomach by a steel hand. I dart my gaze about searching for her: Justine – my new madonna, icon, inner ideal made manifest in the world. But instead my eye is drawn to a dancing couple. With a start I realize it is Viki. She is arm in arm with a thick set man. Her sweetest smile is on him, her large almond eyes alight. She knows where I am sitting. I turn away disgusted with the ploy. I stop looking for Justine, too aware of Viki's proximity. I pick up my small sweating drink, more for something to hold than for the glass's contents, slide off barstool and cross the floor to find the others at the table: a sanctuary. I catch from the corner of my eye Viki smiling triumphant. Does she think she has driven me off? So too territorial.

At the table a chair was free between Dulcie Sassoon and Madeleine. James made a beeline for it. Dulcie was tossing her ragged hair back a wasted look on her face as she laughed at something Jerry Rafferty was saying; there was a mischievous glint to his eye that James knew meant one thing only with Jerry: drink. And lots of it.

Slump down in seat between Madeleine and Dulcie. Cacophony of noises drown out any immediate need for conversation. Red and black colours spin. Still no sight of Justine.

Then she appears: luminous, as though walking alone through an empty room. A still point, as though in a vortex of sound and colour she is standing static in her flowing white dress against a projected backdrop of movement. She does not come straight over to the table; perhaps she has not yet seen it. She moves slightly as though looking for something, clutching her small bag to her chest. She stands still again. Now she is obviously looking about her, suddenly unsure. Then her gaze sweeps the table and falls on James. Her face lights up in a smile and she relaxes. Jauntily she moves over to him and standing behind his chair places a fluttering hand, warm on his shoulder. The warmth spread through James, even to his heart and his head. He looks up but she was looking away as though into a great distance.

Just then Clara and her daughter arrived at the table followed by a dancing retinue of masked followers. People stood up. People sat down. Dulcie was replaced by a masked figure smoking a Black Russian through a long cigarette holder, smoke pouring out mysteriously from through the plastic mouth hole. Justine sat on his lap.

"Strange friends Clara has," said Madeleine leaning over. But before James could reply the music was boosted. Flashing strobe lights raked the floor and the masked figures were dancing, Clara like a goddess at their centre, an enraptured smile fixed on her face. Emily joined her and the worship centered on both mother and daughter. There was a loud crash. Jerry had fallen off his chair. He was clutching an old broken stringed guitar staring up at James in complete surprise. Hands helped him to his feet and he sat back down and attempted to strum his guitar as though he could rival the giant sound system pumping out that night there in Soho.

Justine was heavy on his lap. She twisted round and kissed him, long and slow; the weight of her body on him mitigated by the flow of energy from the kiss. In the dim swirl of bodies surrounding them he had lost track of Viki; lost interest in whether she was scowling or acting or whatever. Her games were for herself now, alone, and he had planted on him a new life, kissing and caressing, her dark eyes swimming towards his soul.

The volume was up, the dancing going wild, Jaks filling up. He pushed Justine gently up then taking her by the hand led her out through the door into the downstairs lobby where he could hear her speak. Still holding her hand he asked:

"Shall we go back to my flat? Fed up with this."

"You go, baby. I wanna dance some more. I join you later. Leave your phone switch on."

She didn't want to come. She did later. Made sense. He felt his body tired. Nothing nicer than to go back and shower and wait for her.

"Yes," he said.

They fell into an embrace. Her mouth on his. Her arms searching. Limbs moving. Then she was gone through the swing doors back into the arena, a swift backward look with her coal black eyes smiling an affirmation.

He climbed the stairs somewhat giddy, retrieved his coat and stepped into the night air.

There was Viki.

Before she saw him there she stood, a certain feline grace lent to her thickening features, a forward jutting, an outer sign of her inner determination. It would have touched him on a deeper level if her drive had not been so caught up in her paranoid battle for survival. Not all her own fault, James reasoned to himself – paranoia being ones worst fears confirmed (or even fears one never even knew one had).

CHAPTER FOURTEEN: THE TWO MUSES 01:15AM

Then she noticed him, standing irresolute, mired in thought, and a slight sneer crept onto her mouth, so his heart lurched and fell a note. James half smiled. He attempted a wave as he moved off and thought he noticed her mouth soften, a hint of panic creep over her eyes. But it was dark (too dark to see). Opposite the tramp had vanished from his alley. James walked to the corner. He looked back. Viki was still stood there but seemingly oblivious to his hovering. He half wanted to go back; to hug her? to be with her? Surely not. The yellow light of a cab for hire was slowly cruising the next street. He lifted an arm to hail it instinctively. As it stopped and he moved off he caught a last glimpse of Viki. But he could tell nothing from it.

The cab lurches away. The image of Viki is still large in my mind even as the streets flow by creating a greater distance every instant between it and the real her. Is she still standing there? She must have moved, even slightly. Time is space, and space time. The cab meter ticks furiously.... and time is money; but is space money? My mind is numb, tired. I let the image of Viki go – lost to time and space... instead a picture of Justine dancing in the club below swims into my mind. Then I change it to make her sit at the bar. I visualize outside Jaks, see the awning flapping in the wind, the street deserted.

The cab swerves and I reach out to steady myself. Shop windows flicker past too fast for me to see what is displayed in their neon lit windows without making an effort to hold an image of one of them still by moving my head as the cab sweeps past. Tiring of this game I lie back on the soft bench seat and listen to the pleasant whirr of the taxi's diesel engine softly humming to me.

It occurred to me that some might consider me a lucky man: two muses; a free choice. But it didn't hit me like that. The park was drifting past on my left, its tall gaunt trees overhanging the wide empty road. I had no feeling of choice. Viki had already rejected me – at any rate she was hardly fighting for me, not that she should... not that she should. On the contrary: she had her own life to live and his part had always in a way been a walk on. Perhaps she would be happy to see the back of me?

Justine was just what was happening, was all; a new thread that was weaving into his existence, a colour that was spreading through the present and into the future. He felt the future an amorphous blob: it could be felt but not apprehended; something one is moving towards: a distant shoreline moving closer, coming into clarity slowly, part separating from part like the pixels of a computer generated image.

He opened his eyes. The park was still rolling past. How long it was. The Spanish gardens with their fountains, then another belt of parkland trees, then the Jacobean Palace at the back – reflections of Diana – and the bulky mansions of Palace Gardens. Then it was all over and here was the cityscape of Notting Hill all urban and lit for the night in a thousand necklaces of light.

Slowly the cab braked to a halt and I hopped out and paid the man.

Searching for my keys. A sudden panic like slivers of ice in my heart and stomach as I cannot find them. Then I feel their familiar hard shape and the feeling subsides. I take a breath to steady myself, head still spinning slightly as I slide the key into the lock, a smooth rasping of metal against metal then feel the slight weight as I turn it. The door swings open and I climb the stairs a weariness on my limbs, a sweat breaking on my brow. I suddenly can't wait to be inside – my cocoon, nest – shed my clothes and throw myself down so my body can stop and my mind float free. At the top of the stairs I fumble my flat door open, throw the keys on the table, pull off my coat and hang it up, pull off my chelsea boots, socks on floor, belt unbuckle, trousers on floor, shirt buttons one by one so slow, cuff buttons, off, finally unencumbered and I pad into the front room feet cooling on the cold floorboards and leaving the lights off throw myself on the sofa, adjust my legs and back, prop up my head and breath a deep sigh of relief. Lie there panting and the ceiling swimming in vortex swirls as my breath slowly slows and stills, the throb at my temples subsiding and a slight sense of nausea melting away. I search for the remote. My hand falls on it but I push it away. Lets watch inner TV.

Visions spill into my mind like the pourings of the ocean. Pictures of the day: Montagu Withnail Smith his cloak billowing in a strangely day for night darkened street as though the sun were eclipsed. But that had not really happened – how much was imagination impinging on reality? images tumbled together, a mix from the day and his imagination, as though he were a painter mixing colours from two palettes. He opened his eyes and looked at the room: shadows playing in the street light, a simulacrum of his mind, the light outside illuminating the inner room, where a shadow could assume the shape of a rabbit, of a hat, a face, an angel, a demon.

Or nothing.

Again a random tumble of images as he closed his eyes. Viki dancing on the floor at Jaks. Madeleine, her soft brown eyes inviting him to converse. Clara holding court to her suitors like some latter day Penelope.

And they swirled into a vortex.

Then I remembered the shower I had thought of having.

I hauled myself off the sofa and stripped naked thinking the while of Justine's promised (promising) return. Wondered how long she would be. The hot water streaming over my re-awakened body seemed also to flush the day away, wash my mind clear. The vortex slowed and stilled under its steady stream; and it was just me, a man called James, standing under a shower the bathroom fan whirring the light illuminating the whole – a small world, a box of a universe; and as I reached for the soap I felt as one for the first time that day.

I rubbed myself down and put on a toweling gown. I made my way to the bedroom as though by instinct and the cat appeared out of nowhere to follow me in. I lay down on the bed the cat curling up next to me, a small warm body pulsing faintly next to mine. I thought of Justine's body soon to come, her warmth so much more encompassing than the cat, her skin so soft, luxuriant, and I wondered that God in his infinite wisdom had created such a being for man; a rare biblical moment for my usual humanistic mode of progressive thinking. The clock read 3:15 – blattering out its digital staccato insistence to my closing eyes.

I must have drifted off for when I opened my eyes again the clock read 3:55. The cat was still leant up against me, her warmth a small presence against me. I stroked her and was rewarded with a wag of her tail that fell with a single thump on the duvet. I remembered Justine. I pushed out of bed my heart pulsing a little.

I walk through and sit down in an armchair still in my bathrobe. Outside the light from the street spills silently into the room illuminating it with a ghostly glow, objects half made out, a patch of wall only bright in the illumination of an invisible lamp.

Twenty-four hours, I say to myself half aloud. I was here twenty four hours ago listening to the same swoosh of a car as it coasted up Campden Hill: only now I was listening for the sound of the doorbell. The cat comes in to join me, mews, then brushes her tail against my leg in a small gesture of affirmation – solidarity? the solidarity of all living things for each other? James wondered. How was all life linked and why? If all was illusion how did time and space exist; then disappear each moment to be reborn? And then as though in a reverie that fell on him like a summer day-dream it suddenly and mysteriously felt as though the day had not existed at all, that he had sat down and dreamt the whole thing and it was still 4:05 in the morning of the night before. It felt most strangely and thrillingly real: as though he had proved to himself that life really is illusion; a trick of the mind – nothing ever happens at all. But then why was he aware of sitting. Had he been sitting here for eternity like a God dreaming the world into existence. For a moment it seemed quite plausible. He half listened for the sound of the same revelers passing down

173

beneath his window that he had heard the night before, as though this would prove his point to him. He was half afraid he would and the point would be proven. Then what? He looked up involuntarily towards the door and was suddenly impatient for the sound of its ring. Where was she? Dancing? Still? Had Viki waylaid her and poisoned her mind against him?... so fragile the mind. "Frailty thy name is woman." He sighed: what's the difference, men and women – surely we are so nearly the same that it makes no odds – a trick of nature, a plaything in the mind of the creator, an oddity not easily to be explained.

James found himself becoming increasingly impatient both with himself and his thoughts. But he just sat there. He had little option. The action was all on Justine's end now. Even the cat had lost interest in him as he sat there waiting for love. "I seek to die now, for love has failed, and passed me by"; he said aloud to himself. After which he fell silent. The fridge began its humming: time was flowing again, and he felt a soft electric charge flow through the atmosphere as in after a storm.

Perhaps the doorbell would never ring.

But then again it just might.

A slow smile spread across his face at this last positive promise – and as he smiled there sounded loud in his ears a ringing, so sudden and familiar that he was both startled and thrown into normality at the same time. He leapt up and almost tripping over the cat raced towards the door as though the hounds of time were snapping at his heals.

Printed in the United Kingdom by
Lightning Source UK Ltd., Milton Keynes
139100UK00002B/1/P

9 780979 598418